Children of

Africa

Also by Louise A. Stinetorf • CHILDREN OF NORTH AFRICA • CHILDREN OF SOUTH AFRICA • ELEPHANT OUTLAW • MUSA THE SHOEMAKER

Children of
Africa

by Louise A. Stinetorf

J. B. Lippincott Company • *Philadelphia* • *New York*

Contents

Camel Boy

Gizeh is just a poor little town in Egypt with a few houses of sun-dried brick and a half dozen camel-hair tents scattered here and there on its outskirts. All the people who live in Gizeh have one occupation—or just about one occupation. They guide and feed the people from all over the world who come to look at the Pyramids and the Sphinx.

Every day in the year, weekdays and Sundays, dry and rainy season, such visitors come out to Gizeh from Cairo, which is only a few miles away. Nasir had been used to these people from the four corners of the earth from the day he was able to toddle out-

7

side the family tent and watch the first automobiles roll up almost before the sky was red in the east. But as well as he knew them, he never quite got over the feeling that they were queer and not at all like ordinary folk—not like himself or his father and mother and baby sister, for instance. When a car drove up, there was no telling how the people who stepped out of it would be dressed. There were Europeans whose men wore trousers and whose women wore skirts. And there were Chinese whose men wore skirts and whose women wore trousers. Then the next car would be full of American women, with nothing between their foolish heads and the blazing African sun. And right after them might be several men from India, with yards and yards of the finest cloth wrapped around their skulls.

But regardless of how they dressed, or what language they spoke, they all behaved the same way. They all chattered and chattered, and craned their necks and looked at the Pyramids. Then Nasir's father and the other men who lived in tents also, rented them camels to ride around the Pyramids. Nasir could never understand why anyone wanted to ride around the Pyramids. Each side was exactly the same as the other. Yet everyone who came to look at the great piles of stone, hired a camel and rode around the Pyramids—no matter how hard it rained or how hot the sun.

They were such fools, these people! Every one of them! A driver could ask almost any price he wanted for the use of a mangy, sick, flea-bitten old camel; and these people paid it. Sometimes they argued a little bit. But they were little children when it came to bargaining. And if they did not pay the first price asked, they paid only five or ten cents less. More than that, one only had to tell them that one had a sick wife, or a sick child, or that the camels they were riding belonged to the sheik, and they poured extra money into one's hands at the end of the ride! Then, if they took one's picture, they gave one still more money.

They were very curious people, Nasir thought. Oh, undoubtedly, they were past all understanding, these people who came from far-away lands to look at Egypt's ancient tombs!

Some of these people climbed the sides of the Pyramids, clambering over the huge blocks of stone to the very top. All they could do, after they had sat in the blazing sun for a while, was to clamber right down again over the same huge steps of stone.

Now and then there would be a man who clambered up one of the Pyramids at night, and who would sit on the top in the moonlight. When this happened, someone had to watch him so it could be reported to the police if he fell off. That was how Nasir met Mr. Thompson.

Mr. Thompson was tall and thin, and Nasir knew as soon as he first saw him that he was either American or European because he wore trousers and a coat made of good woolen cloth of a drab color. Mr. Thompson hired a camel just like everyone else who came in his car, and rode around the Pyramids and Sphinx. He also climbed to the top of the largest Pyramid.

But as soon as that was over, Mr. Thompson began to behave differently from the average visitor. When Nasir told him that he was riding one of the sheik's camels, he didn't seem at all impressed. Instead, he remarked that the sheik should feed his camels better, and that he ought to treat them for mange. Then Nasir said that his wife and children were all sick—this had never failed to get a generous donation before! Mr. Thompson merely looked at Nasir sharply and suggested that he seemed pretty young to have a wife and children; but that if it were true that a boy of twelve did have a wife and children who were sick, he should call a doctor! Then Nasir suggested that Mr. Thompson take his picture, and Mr. Thompson merely asked, "Why?" When Mr. Thompson settled for his camel, he gave Nasir the amount one Arab would have paid another.

When the visitors piled into the big cars at last and left for Cairo, Mr. Thompson was not with them. He had bought some bread and barbecued meat from a Gizeh street peddler, and he was calmly eating his supper under a palm tree.

That evening, when the moon came up, Nasir saw him start to climb the biggest Pyramid all alone. The police officer had not come and asked Nasir's father to watch the stranger. But Nasir knew that it was dangerous for one unused to clambering over the great blocks of stone to try to do it all by himself, and especially at night. So the boy settled down to watch.

The moon came up and it was almost as clear and bright as daytime. And the stars twinkled. It was as though they were merry and chuckling to themselves at someone. Out on the desert a little fox yelped and the dogs of Gizeh barked. Nasir's head grew heavier and heavier.

"Whoooooooaa!" was the next sound Nasir heard, and there was Mr. Thompson bending over him. Of course Nasir didn't know what "Whooooaa!" meant, for an Arab doesn't say *whoa* to a camel. Nasir did know, however, that he had fallen asleep and that the stranger had come down off the Pyramid safely and had stumbled over him.

"Did I hurt you?" Mr. Thompson asked. Now, Nasir understood English, for most of the people who came to visit the Pyramids spoke English, and he had heard it ever since he was able to toddle after a camel. But Mr. Thompson was speaking Arabic,

Nasir's own language—not pidgin Arabic, which even the most ignorant peasant would have laughed at, but fine, fluent classical Arabic such as the students at the American University at Cairo used. Nasir just looked at this man.

"I'm sorry," the man said. Then instead of going away, he sat down beside Nasir and started staring at the Pyramid again.

"It's beautiful, isn't it?" he murmured.

Then Nasir stared at the Pyramid, too, and wondered how anyone could have such a queer notion of beauty. It was big! Yes! Bigger than a thousand village houses. Bigger than ten thousand village houses! But even so, it was only blocks of stone with little heaps of desert sand blown into the cracks and crannies.

"What do you see when you look at the Pyramids, my boy?" Mr. Thompson asked suddenly, and then looked at Nasir as carefully as Nasir looked at the Pyramid.

"Well, there's stone, and sand, and dust. And bits of moss on the shady side," Nasir answered in Arabic.

"Don't you see anything else?"

Nasir peered carefully, squinting through his dark lashes.

"No," he finally answered gravely.

"Do you know what I see when I look at the

Pyramid?" Mr. Thompson asked.

Of course, there was no telling what a queer foreigner ever saw, or explaining what he did, Nasir thought. But he didn't say so. He didn't say anything at all, and Mr. Thompson went on without waiting for a reply.

"I see men and women who knew much more about many things—building, for instance—than we do today. Men and women who plowed with a crooked stick, yet conquered the desert and made it 'bloom like a rose.' Who had no compasses, yet found their way across the trackless sands. Who worked without our tools and created art objects we can't duplicate today. Who had no machinery and yet mined gold and precious gems from the earth. Whose boats were like cockleshells, and yet who set out for strange new territories unafraid. Who had no telescopes and yet who charted the courses of the stars. Who used slabs of wet clay for paper and wrote books on them. Who . . ."

Mr. Thompson's voice went on and on, and Nasir stared at him in amazement. Finally he squirmed.

"Don't ask me how they did all these things," Mr. Thompson said to Nasir as though the boy had questioned him. "I don't know—yet! Maybe I'll never know! But this summer I'm going to go into these Pyramids and hunt for the clay tablets which will answer some of the world's questions about the men who built these huge tombs."

The two were quiet for a little while and then the man went on, "I'll need a lot of people to help me. Do you want a job?"

All that summer Nasir worked for Mr. Thompson. Sometimes he carried water. Sometimes he washed dried mud and dust from stone tablets and pieces of clay jars. Sometimes he sifted the fine dust and sand carried out of the Pyramids for bits of beads and jewels. Other times he just followed Mr. Thompson around and listened to him talk about the people who had lived in Egypt three or four thousand years ago. By the end of the long Egyptian summer, before Mr. Thompson packed up his notebooks and instruments and tents and went away, Nasir, too, was able to look at the Pyramids in the moonlight and see strange things.

"What do you see when you look at this Pyramid?" Nasir asked a visitor one day as he led the camel on which she was riding.

It was a rainy day, and cold for Egypt; and the visitor was cross.

"Oh, it's just another pile of big stones," she answered shortly.

"It's more than that," Nasir maintained. Then, when the woman looked at him, he went on: "It's

the record written in stone of a race of men who have never been equaled. Look at it carefully, lady! Come back tonight and look at it by moonlight. Then, if you will use your imagination, you will see thousands, yet, tens of thousands of slaves—your ancestors, maybe!—working for my forefathers. This pile of rock is the tomb of men who knew much more about some things—building, for instance—than we do today. Men and women who plowed with a crooked stick and yet conquered the desert and made it 'bloom like a rose.' Who had no compasses and yet found their way across the trackless sands. Who had no machinery and yet mined gold and precious gems. Who set out for strange lands in boats almost as fragile as lotus flowers. Who charted the courses of the planets without telescopes. Who wrote books on the bark of weeds and on slabs of wet clay. Those folk who see here only a huge pile of rock are ignorant indeed!"

That evening a tourist in a Cairo hotel told a group of fellow travelers about a strange little camel boy out at the Pyramids who recited Egyptian history like a poet.

"I was so amazed and so pleased I gave him ten times too much for a tip," she confessed.

One tourist spoke to another about Nasir. Here was a little guide who did not pretend to have a sick wife and children or the sheik's camels in order to beg money. Neither did he tease to have his picture taken. He did not invent fanciful names for his camel, such as "Whiskeysoda" and "Ginricky" in order to amuse his tourists. Instead he told them what was inside the sealed doors of the huge tombs, and strange things about the lives of the men who had built them.

Nasir became the most popular camel boy at the Pyramids. The tips he received were large and when Mr. Thompson returned the following summer, Nasir felt almost a rich man. Again for a whole season he carried water, washed clay tablets and bits of broken pottery and sifted the dust and sand carried out of the tombs.

But that fall he did not guide camel-mounted tourists around the Pyramids. Instead he sat behind a desk at a mission school in Cairo. There people from Mr. Thompson's country taught him all they knew about his forefathers who had made slaves of their own ancestors.

Their Heads
in the Sun

Aida's legs were very tired this morning. She wished that they owned an ox to tread upon the water wheel. Over and over again she and her brother had been climbing to make the big wheel turn around and around so that the water from the Nile would keep pouring from the buckets into channels of the little cotton field. The hot African sun had baked the earth, and the plants were thirsty . . .

Near the palm tree was a bit of restful shade and a place to rest her weary legs; but she knew that, if the wheel stopped, her mother and father would stop their weeding and call for them to go on with their work. 'Round and 'round went the wheel, and the perspiration poured down from Aida's forehead—on down past the tattoo mark in front of her right ear. The earrings in her ears looked strange with the dress she wore. It was a long dress, made of coarse dark material, dragging in the back, in order to wipe out her footsteps. For Aida believed that should anyone step in her footprints, it would bring her very bad luck.

She looked at her little brother closely, and thanked Allah that He did not want a scarecrow. Aida's mother had told her of her other two little brothers whom Allah had taken because they were so beautiful. He had taken them to Heaven to be with Him, long before Aida was born. But Allah had not noticed this little brother. His mother had hidden his good looks by shaving patches on his head the very day he was born. Now she kept cutting his hair in helter-skelter tufts all over his head so that he would look like a scarecrow! Allah had left this little boy with his thankful parents on the earth. He, too, looked very tired—and the funny little tufts of hair were wet with perspiration, now as midday approached.

The sun was so high overhead that Aida could scarcely see even a few inches of shadow in any direction. It was time to have lunch in the shade of the palm trees nearby. In a few minutes, that seemed like very long minutes to Aida, her mother called to

19

them. Her father had stopped his hoeing, and now sat there eating a piece of unleavened bread with the family. Aida munched on a handful of dates. She could hear her brother's teeth crunching some nuts as he crept up beside his father and lay down. They had all worked hard this day, just as on the other days when the plants were thirsty and the weeds seemed to grow faster than the plants. Soon the father and the little brother were fast asleep. It would be a long time before they awakened under these palm trees in the garden. Although the sun was hottest now, Aida was not sleepy. She did not feel as warm now as she had while working on the *sakieh*, which was her name for the water wheel.

Above her head, the leaves of the palm trees were very still. She squinted at them through her long black eyelashes and thought of how they would wave gently to and fro in the evening breeze. Her eyes wandered, looking lazily now at the pile of fresh palm leaves her father had cut down before he stretched out to sleep. The leaves were long and green and very soft. She began to tear the leafy fronds into narrow widths for her father and brother to twist into good strong rope. Her mother was weaving a basket now, using the heavy mid-ribs of the palm leaves—strong and sturdy. Here by the Nile River the palm trees brought them so many things. Aida thought of yesterday when her mother

had said that there was once a time when there were no palm trees on the earth. She had begged for a story then, for Aida's mother, like so many Egyptian mothers, and fathers, too, loved to tell stories. She had spoken in that faraway tone of voice that Aida loved to hear, for then there was always an old tale to follow. But the shadows had been growing bigger yesterday, and it had been too late for Mother to start. Today Aida said to her mother, "Mother, what would a village do without palm trees? You said yesterday that once upon a time there were no palm trees on the earth."

"Ah, yes," her mother smiled, looking at Aida with a faraway gleam in her eyes, "it was in those days of so long ago that people were very poor, very poor indeed." She spoke softly to her daughter who waited patiently for the rest of the story. They must not wake the sleeping father and the little son.

"Palm trees were a gift from God," she began, "and the old men tell the story of a village where the people were very, very poor—oh! much poorer than we are today. They never had enough to eat, and men and women were so hungry sometimes that it was hard for them not to look enviously at the bread that went into their children's mouths. They never had enough to wear so that the women were ashamed to work in the fields where people could see them; and so it was that their menfolk had all the heavy work of the harvesting to do alone. And the garments of the men were so thin and poor that when a cruel wind blew off the desert by day, their bodies were scorched. And when a bitter wind blew down out of the Libyan Mountains by night, they shivered with the cold."

"I wouldn't like that at all!" Aida remarked positively.

"Neither did these poor people," her mother added, "but then they couldn't help themselves! One day a poor man who had been working in his garden patch all morning, sat down by a pool of water to eat his lunch. He couldn't sit in the shade of a palm tree because, of course, there weren't any palm trees. So he sat in the blazing sun and unwrapped the crust of bread his wife had given him for his noonday meal. As he broke off a bit and started to put it into his mouth, he heard a feeble cry. It was hardly more than a whisper.

" 'Water! Water! For mercy's sake, give me water!' he heard someone say.

"The farmer looked across the little pool and there was the thinnest and raggedest man he had ever seen. Much thinner and—oh! ever so much more ragged than himself."

"Was he so ragged you could see right through his clothes?" Aida asked. "Ragged like old Ismail, the beggar?"

"Yes, oh yes," her mother answered. "Even ragged than old Ismail! And he was dirty, too. The dust was caked on his sandals and the bottom part of his robe, showing he had traveled far. The farmer had not seen nor heard anyone approaching, but that was not strange because he had been busy thinking of his wife and children at home. He had been wishing there were some way a man might keep up his strength so he could work in the fields without eating. Then he would not need to bring a crust of bread to the fields with him—even a very small one—and his children could have it instead."

"It would be dreadful to be that hungry, wouldn't it?" Aida interrupted again.

"Yes!" her mother answered patiently. "The man's crust wasn't nearly so much as anyone working hard in the fields should have had. And while he looked at it and wished it were much more, the man heard the feeble cry for water—and there the stranger was! He had fallen and had crawled the last few steps to the pool. There, with the fingers of one hand touching the water, his strength had failed him and he could go no farther.

"'Water!' he begged piteously. 'In the Name of God, the most merciful, give me water!'

"The farmer could see that the stranger's lips were cracked and bleeding, and his tongue was almost black. It was very clear that he had not drunk for a long time. The farmer laid his crust of bread on the ground and scooped up water in his cupped palms and poured it over the man's burned face and into his mouth. Again and again and again he scooped up water from the pool until the man could sit up.

"It was then that the stranger noticed the bread lying on the ground, and stretched out his hand for it.

" 'Bread! Give me some of your bread!' he begged as eagerly as he had asked for the water.

"But the farmer hesitated. He was hungry himself and he had worked hard all morning in the hot sun. He needed the food to keep up his strength so he could work and grow grain for his family. He held the crust in one hand and in the other the small piece he had broken off before he heard the stranger's first cry for water. If he had not needed the food for himself, he would have left it at home for his wife and children. He looked at the stranger, and the man's eyes followed every movement of the hand holding the bread—like the eyes of a hungry child.

" 'I have not eaten—I do not know when it was I ate last,' the man faltered."

"Was he as hungry as the farmer's children?" Aida wanted to know.

"Much, much hungrier! The farmer could see that, for the man was very thin. He was even thinner than the farmer's own wife, or the farmer himself.

His arms above his wrists were no bigger around than a child's and the knuckles of his fingers stood out like knobs. The sockets of his eyes were deep and the skin stretched tight across his cheek bones.

"But the farmer thought to himself: 'If I give my children's food to this stranger, they, too, will look at me with hollow eyes and their flesh will waste away.' And the farmer turned his face toward the pool of water because he could not bear to see the misery and longing in the other man's eyes. Then he gave a start of surprise. The pool which had been muddy and covered with a green scum a few minutes before was now fresh and crystal clear. The farmer could see his face in it as clearly as though it were a mirror.

" 'I beseech you, give me a little bread,' the stranger begged again. 'God is most merciful to those who are charitable to the needy and helpless.'

"The farmer remembered those verses in the Koran, which read:

'Righteousness is in those who . . . giveth unto orphans, and the needy and the stranger . . . who are constant at prayer and giveth alms . . . who behave themselves patiently in adversity, and in hardship. . . . These are they who are true and who fear God.'

" 'Perhaps,' the farmer thought, almost speaking to himself, 'perhaps this man also has a wife and children. Perhaps they are hungry and are waiting for him to bring them food. If I do not feed him, he is too weak to look elsewhere and he will surely die. Then what will happen to his loved ones? If I feed him, who knows how many lives I may save?'

"The farmer dropped on his knees beside the stranger and put a crumb of bread in his mouth. The man ate greedily, bite by bite. It seemed to the farmer that he grew plumper and stronger by the second. At last there was only one crumb left. The stranger got to his feet, and the farmer thought he had never seen quite so handsome a man. His face shone, and he no longer trembled from weakness. Even his clothes no longer looked ragged, but were clean and soft as though they had been bought in a good shop.

"Then the stranger did a curious thing. He scooped a shallow hole in the mud on the bank of the pool, placed the last remaining bit of bread in the hole, and carefully covered it over with good soil. As he patted the ground, a little green shoot appeared and grew and grew and grew before the farmer's awe-struck eyes. The stem reached toward heaven, and the trunk thickened until it was as big around as a man's body.

"Then out of its top burst a crown of green leaves and a great cluster of red and black dates. The shade cast by the leaves was cool and good, and the farmer liked it. Some of the fruit fell to the ground. The farmer ate a handful of it and it, too, was sweet and good. He felt strength course through his veins again. Here was food, good food too, much better than dry bread, that he could take to his wife and children!

"The farmer was very happy and he turned to the stranger to thank him, but there was no one there. There were not even any footsteps where he might have stood. But there was the palm tree with its sweet fruit and with its leaves making cool shade— the very first palm tree in all the world. And all the palm trees forever after are just like it—unhappy unless they can stand with their roots in the water and their heads thrust into the sun."

Aida sighed because the story was done.

"Life would be very different and hard without the fruit and shade of the palm tree. Would it not, Mother?" she asked.

Her mother paused a moment and glanced out across the Nile River, the half-finished basket of palm leaves resting in her lap.

"The palm tree is God's promise that He will feed and shelter man as long as man keeps His commandments," she answered softly.

Snake Charmer

In Cairo, like every other place in the world, mothers clean house. Then, just like every other place in the world, there is a great orgy of sweeping, dusting, scrubbing, and general scurrying about—and no one seems to have time for the children. Jane felt deserted when her father, who worked with other Englishmen in an office downtown, had left the house earlier than usual that morning, for even Nurse was hurrying from room to room, with a cloth tied over her hair.

In the house, Jane got under everybody's feet. And it wasn't a nice place to be anyway, for there was a mop or a pail or a frantic house boy in every corner, it seemed. So there was just nothing for her to do! She couldn't go calling on her friends, or to the parks, or museums, or anywhere else for that matter; for in Cairo no little English girl sets foot in the street without her nurse, stiff in white uniform, beside her.

That left only the garden, and Jane wandered out there to see if the pale blue of the plumbago still hung on the trellises, if the great poinsettias of the hedge had put out any red blossoms yet, or if the giant geraniums were all dried up or not since yesterday.

But as Jane started down the stone steps, the cook shouted the one Arabic word which may mean almost anything under the sun:

"Y'Allah! *Y'ALLAH!!*"

Strangely enough, no one ever misunderstands what is meant. Perhaps it is because of the tone of voice used. Anyway, Jane froze in her tracks, scarcely daring to turn her head to look at the cook.

"Y'Allah! Bedish!"—Stop! Go Back!

There was no disobeying that voice, and Jane scurried up the steps and onto the porch. There she turned and looked across to the little balcony opening off the kitchen where the cook stood. The servant waved his hands toward the flower beds.

"Yesterday, or the day before yesterday, or before that, maybe"—no Arab will ever name a definite date or time if he can avoid doing so—"sometime anyway, an adder—she come into the garden. She like it here and she bring her wife. And now, who knows where to step? Or to pluck a flower? Or what lies beneath the leaves of the salad greens?"

The cook never used but two personal pronouns: "me" and "she," but Jane understood him perfectly and a shiver ran through her. Everyone who has ever lived in Egypt knows how hard it is to tell an adder from a little ridge of sand. Everyone knows how easily and quickly that little ridge can whip itself upward and around a bare ankle and sink its long wicked teeth into the bare flesh. And everyone also knows that for everybody but the very strongest, this means pain and discomfort for a long time.

Jane looked across at the cook and shivered. She clenched her toes inside her slippers and the muscles of her calves tensed as though she were ready to run away, although she knew she was safe on the porch. An adder will not leave the sand.

"Does Father know about the adders?" Jane asked.

"Master no know," the cook answered. "Master go to office. Me send for snake charmer."

Jane had heard of these men who could make reptiles obey them. They are often talked about at gatherings of English officials or American business-men in Cairo. Nearly everyone laughed at them, Jane knew.

But there was always someone in a group who

would remark, "Well, I'm not sure they're fakes. Some of these natives can do strange things, you know!"

Father had been one of the men who always laughed at the stories of snake charmers, but then, he had never had adders in his garden before. Jane wondered what he would do if he were at home. But he was at the office and the cook had sent for the native snake charmer, and now he was keeping watch to see that no one entered the garden until it was cleared of snakes. Jane pulled up a carved stool and sat down to wait for the snake charmer. Maybe it wouldn't be such a dull morning after all.

Presently he came—in through the back gate and up the walk to the kitchen balcony he strode.

"Yesterday, or the day before yesterday, or before that maybe," the cook began excitedly, "sometime anyway, an adder she come into the garden. She like it here and she bring her wife. Now who dares step on the walk or put his hand among the vegetables or flowers?"

The snake charmer looked contemptuously at the cook.

"I dare!" he said shortly. He had no more than glanced at the ground as he shuffled his flapping sandals along the walk.

"You catch snakes?" the cook begged.

"If Allah is satisfied with the price," the magician

answered as unconcernedly as though he weren't even interested in the job.

The cook dropped some coins into the snake charmer's hand. He counted them and put them in a little bag dangling from his belt. Then he looked the cook calmly in the face.

"That is baksheesh (charity) for my donkey," he remarked.

The cook handed over a few more coins. And more! And more!

"Baksheesh! Baksheesh!" the magician kept repeating, meaning that the cook was trying to hire him for as little money as he would drop in a beggar's cup. But finally he seemed satisfied, and then he set to work.

First of all he walked up and down every path in the garden until he had found a spot that suited him. Then he unrolled a little carpet, sat down upon it, and untied a bundle he had brought with him and arranged its contents about him—a clay pot here, a pair of light bamboo sticks there, and a heavy club in front of him. At last everything was ready.

The snake charmer picked up the heavy club and beat on the top of the ground. Then he laid his ear to the earth and listened carefully. Jane and the cook waited and watched breathlessly. Nothing happened and the magician thumped the earth again with his club. Once more he laid his ear to the ground and listened. This time he appeared satisfied.

Then he settled back on his haunches and pulled a shepherd's pipe out of his belt. This curious little instrument is made of four reeds of different lengths bound together. Each reed has two or three holes in it and can sound two or three different notes. It is the sort of pipe shepherds all over the Middle East play—a musical instrument that has not changed in the last three of four thousand years.

The magician began piping a monotonous little tune that reminded Jane of a little child crying in the night. Gently at first he swayed his body back and forth from side to side. Then faster and faster and farther and farther he bent until he almost touched the ground on either side. The wide sleeves brushed the sand as he swayed.

Jane could never have told how long he played. When he stopped, she realized that she, too, had been swaying to the music. The silence was like the opening of a door—or the untying of a tight belt. Jane could breathe again freely. She looked across at the cook. He was wiping the perspiration from his neck.

The magician dropped his pipes in his lap and picked up the bamboo sticks. Swiftly and delicately, like an artist touching paint to a canvas, he leaned over forward and picked up a small sand-colored snake from the ground in front of him and dropped

it into the jar. Jane could hear the cook sigh with relief.

Again the magician began playing, swaying gently back and forth, and a second time he picked up a little light brown snake with the bamboo sticks. The cook started down the steps, but the magician, without looking at him, held up his hand.

"There are three snakes in the garden," he said shortly and began playing once more.

Softly and gently the weak little tune shrilled up and down monotonously until Jane felt she could surely stand it no longer. The magician must have been mistaken. There could be no more snakes in the garden! But the snake charmer was right. At long last he tucked his pipes back in his belt and picked up another adder so tiny and short it looked like a piece of dirty string.

Then he covered up the jar holding the three snakes and tied his club and bamboo sticks back into a bundle. But the cook did not start down the steps again until the man had beckoned to him.

Jane also walked down the stone steps, off the porch, and into the garden now with all the confidence in the world. If the snake charmer said there were no more snakes there—then, there were no more snakes there! She was sure of that.

In a few days she had forgotten all about the whole affair—forgot, that is, until she heard Father read from the cook's account book one evening:

"To the snake charmer for ridding the garden of three adders. .... 4 shillings.
"To the snake charmer as baksheesh for his donkey. .... 1 shilling.

"Adders! Adders!" Father almost shouted. "Those poisonous little snakes in our garden? Why didn't somebody tell *me?*"

"What would you have done?" asked Mother.

"Well! Well—"

That was about all the reply Father ever made, for he knew—and everybody else knew—that neither he nor any of his English or American friends could have gotten the snakes out of his garden. He knew that no matter what he said, the cook would have sent for the snake charmer anyway, just as soon as he had left the house.

Jane wondered if she could make a snake appear by playing on a set of shepherd's pipes. She would like to try it—if only she had a set of shepherd's pipes. And knew how to play on them!

The Marble Hand

Cletis was a curious boy of Tunisia who halfway believed in fairies. That is, he really knew there are no such things as sprites and elves and gnomes. But all to himself he pretended to believe in them. It was good fun, and good company when he was all alone in the deep waters off the harbor of Sfax. Just so long as one didn't tell older folks who might laugh, it was a great comfort to pretend that wonderful things were going to happen. And the most wonderful thing of all was that they sometimes did happen!

Cletis used to pretend that some day, while he was searching for sponges deep down under the water, a beautiful fairy would come out from behind a seaweed and hold out her hand to him and lead him to his heart's desire. He liked the sound of those two words—heart's desire. When he used them, he felt it was all right to wish for something he knew—he was positively certain—that he would never get.

His heart's desire was a boat of his very own. Not so big as the one his father sailed in, of course, but a good sturdy craft of his own that he could sail out to the sponge beds where the other sponge fishermen anchored. If he owned his own boat, he would not have to give up to the man he worked for all of the sponges he gathered. He could keep them himself and he could sell them in the market place. And he would not have to be content with earning only a few pennies a day.

Of course, Cletis was really not big enough to have a boat of his own, but he didn't realize that. Perhaps it was because he was small that he halfway believed that down under the waves some day he would look up and see his fairy, and that then she would find a boat for him.

Cletis's father was a fisherman who fished for fish instead of sponges. Before he had come to Sfax on the Tunisian coast, he had lived on the island of Samos, in the Aegean Sea. He had been a fisherman for fish there, too. He had sailed his boat out into the sea each day and, if there were plenty of fish, had seined the blue waters and piled his catch from the big net into his boat until it could hold no more. Then he had pulled up his anchor, unfurled the sail, and made for home.

Then came a time when he had had to watch the shores of the islands among which he sailed as carefully as he watched the wind and water and his nets. For the Turks who lived to the east of the island of Samos were making war on the Greeks at that time, burning homes and robbing churches and killing what men they could. Of course if they caught a fisherman—well, it was just too bad for whoever happened to be on his boat, and for his wife and children and parents back on the island.

So for a long time Cletis's father had had to fish with one hand on the tiller and one on his nets. He didn't dare drop anchor or furl his sails, for whenever he sighted a big black boat flying the Star and Crescent—which is the Turkish flag—he had to be able to make a run for his life at a moment's notice, tacking back and forth among the islands to spoil the Turkish gunners' aim.

Of course he hadn't caught many fish that way. And the people of Samos had had less and less money to spend for fish as the Turks had destroyed more and more villages and raided more and more of their homes and churches and market places. Finally, matters got so bad that whenever Cletis's father brought any fish home with him, he had to give them to his hungry neighbors. Of course that meant that Cletis's father had less and less money to spend for food himself.

The family usually had fish, but growing children need something more than that. They need olives and olive oil, and bread and fruit and good goat's milk. But the Turks had burned the grain as it stood in the fields. They had chopped down the grape-vines, and the lemon and fig and olive trees. And they had driven off most of the goats.

"Soon they will burn the roof over *our* heads, too," Cletis's mother had wailed one night as news of a new attack came to them.

"They will steal our icons," she went on. An icon is a holy image or picture a Greek Christian kisses when he prays. A good family would never be with-out an icon.

Cletis's father had looked at his wife and children; and he knew that it was not the loss of his icons, or his house, or trees and grapevines, or goats that worried him the most. He was a thrifty man who had worked hard as long as he could remember, but there was nothing he had ever bought with money that was half so precious as the wife and children God had given him.

One morning not long after that, Cletis's father had not gone out to fish. Men and women on the streets told one another that the Turkish land troops were coming nearer and that almost every island hid at least one Turkish boat with big guns on it. So Cletis's father stayed at home. All day long he worked in the garden and fields, making cuttings of the grapevines, and digging up small olive and lemon trees, and packing them in wet wool. In the house his wife packed all the linen and pots and pans and dishes in big chests. Then everything was carried on board Cletis's father's boat, even to the goats and a pig or two, and stored away. When evening fell the family said good-bye to a quiet little group of neighbors, hoisted anchor, and sailed out through and beyond the islands of the Aegean into the Mediterranean Sea.

Cletis's father had known that out there, no matter in what direction one sailed, he would come to land. Of course if one sailed directly east, he would come to Turkey, which would never do. But anywhere else he might land and there he could surely make a home for himself and catch fish in the sea to feed his family as he had always done.

Now, Cletis never tired of hearing his father tell of that trip. He remembered very little of it himself, for he was scarcely more than a baby then. Sometimes it rained and they all huddled below decks with the goats and pigs. But usually the sun shone and his father and mother sat on deck and the children played. After they got over being afraid that Turkish sailors might hear them, they even sang songs and were quite merry.

A soft wind blew most of the time, but since it was *from* the east and not toward it, nobody worried about that. About a week after leaving Samos, the family neared a low, sandy shore and in a little while came in sight of a small town. There were nets spread out to dry on the tops of the dazzling white houses, so Cletis's father knew he was among fisher folk and he sailed into the harbor of Sfax.

He sold his boat and bought a little house and a bit of land. And after he and his wife had planted the vines and seedlings which were unwithered and healthy in their wet wool, Cletis's father got a job as a fisherman on one of the boats that sailed out into the Mediterranean each day.

Cletis's father soon found out, however, that most of the boats did not go out after fish. They went out after sponges that grew thick and big on the floor of the sea all up and down the coast by the little town of Sfax. To gather—or fish for—sponges one grasped a trident, or three-pronged stick in one hand, a large net bag with a few stones in it for weight in the other, took a deep breath, and stepped out of his boat into the water. Down, down he sank until he came to the shallow bottom, where the sponges grew.

Then he had to work fast. He pried the sponges

loose from the sand and rock with his trident, and put them into his bag. When the bag was full—or when he could hold his breath no longer—he threw the stones in his bag away and floated up to the surface of the sea. There his comrades helped him back into the boat and emptied his bag while he lay on the deck and rested before he stepped off into the sea again.

It was work that it was best to learn to do while very young. So it wasn't many years before Cletis was going out in a boat with the other small boys and a few old men and learning how to hold his breath, how to breathe out under water without strangling, how to tell a sponge from coral and seaweed, and everything else he should know to make him a good sponge fisherman. He had good lungs, strong arms and legs, and keen eyes, and he learned very quickly. Naturally, he was a little proud of himself!

Cletis's father, however, was not particularly pleased. He had worked hard and saved his money, and always dreamed of having a boat of his own again. When his son boasted a little of how deep he had dived that day, how long he had stayed under the water, and how many sponges he had brought up, his father seldom said anything. But Cletis's mother knew that an old saying of Samos fishermen was running through his head: "A son's place is in his father's boat." Of course Cletis's father didn't actually have a boat yet, but the whole family watched the little horde of pennies and small pieces of silver grow, and they all planned for the time when he would have one. Cletis knew that when that time came his father would expect him to give up sponge fishing. Much as he disliked the thought, the boy knew he would have to become a fisherman as his father before him. If only he could do something to help his father get a boat, then perhaps his father would not insist that he give up sponge gathering.

Of course Cletis's father could never dive for sponges himself. He had been a grown man when he came to Sfax; and while he swam as all fishermen do, he couldn't hold his breath or open his eyes under water. He didn't know how to make himself sink softly and gently, feet first, to the bottom of the sea. He didn't know what currents were down there, or even what a live sponge looks like.

The sponge as it is sold across counters in stores is the skeleton of thousands of tiny animals. They are very simple creatures with no hands, feet, hearts, heads—nothing but a bit of nerve network and slime. Under water they are beautiful, but as soon as they are brought up out of the water all their lovely colors fade and they become dark and slick and ugly. That was the only way Cletis's father had ever seen them. So he didn't quite understand why his son took so much pride in the sponges he brought up, or why he took so little interest in his father's work. Sometimes they argued a little of an evening.

"There is no joy like battling with a tuna on the end of your line," his father would say. "While you—you walk around and pick up sponges. You might as well pick up pebbles on the beach."

Cletis didn't dare tell his father that there was struggle and victory on the sea's floor, also. That he must keep an eye out for the dark green of the moray eel. That he must know how to hide himself among the sponges and coral—when a shadow glided over the dim sea bed and he looked up and saw a big whale belly above him! That the sharp prongs of his trident had other uses than the prying up of sponges! If his father had suspected for one moment that there was any danger in sponge fishing, he would have forbidden his son ever to dive again.

But he didn't know, and because he realized that life was different in some ways in Sfax from what it had been on the island of Samos, he did not compel Cletis to give up sponge fishing as he might have done. Instead, whenever his son talked of the future and what he was going to do when he was grown up and a man, his father would listen for a while and then ask him if he thought he could ever bring up enough sponges to pay for a good boat.

"In sunlight there is gold, and in moonlight there is
silver on the top of the waves;
But nobody knows what sleeps in the depths
below."

Cletis's father quoted an old poem. He meant, of
course, that he could sell the gold-and-silver-scaled
fish he caught for another kind of gold and silver in
the market place. And he tried to hint to Cletis that
there might be so little money in diving for sponges
that a boy could never hope to save enough money
to buy his own boat.

Cletis, however, thought differently of the old
saying, ". . . but nobody knows what sleeps in the
depths below." He had learned to walk on the
ocean's floor and he knew that all the colors of the
rainbow lurked in the depths and shimmered past
him.

"When I haul my nets up out of the water," his
father would say, "I haul food and comfort for my
family on board. And what do you bring up out of
the depths? Grey, slimy, stinking sponges that sell
for only a few cents."

"There is beauty down there!" Cletis would answer hotly. "Someday—someday I'll prove that to
you!" But in his heart he was afraid he would never
be able to do that. If only sometime he could find
something on the ocean floor that looked as beautiful
in the sunlight as it did in the dim green depths, he

knew his father would begin to understand.

He began peering about him when he dived for sponges. And whenever he saw anything delicate or graceful or full of color, he brought it up with him. Usually the colors faded or the fronds drooped and tangled, or the slime began to smell pretty badly before he could carry his treasure home to show to his father. It discouraged him until he noticed that his mother was using the lumps of coral he picked up now and then to outline her flower beds and garden paths. Then he began to keep an eye out for odd and graceful shapes to bring to her.

Sometimes a lump looked like a head or a foot or a heart. Only roughly like a head or a foot or a heart, of course; but nearly enough so that a boy who wanted to believe in fairies could pretend. Sometimes he made believe that the waves had broken his own particular fairy to pieces—the one who was going to lead him to his boat, that is. He would have to find all the parts and put them back together again. When he had done that, she would hold out her hand to him and say:

"Cletis, my boy, I have been held a prisoner by these sands for hundreds of years, and now you have rescued me."

Cletis wasn't quite sure whether he should sink on one knee before her or just how he should tell her that he was happy to have gotten her body together for her again. Of course, one doesn't really save a fairy's life because a fairy just lives on and on, no matter into how many pieces she may be broken. That is, the fairy that one makes up just to please oneself!

Of one thing he was sure. His fairy would say to him, "What would you rather have more than anything else in all the world?"

And he would answer, "A boat! A sponge fisherman's boat, if you please!"

She would please, of course. Fairies are very obliging that way. She would take him by the hand and lead him around a sponge bank or across a reef or behind a big patch of seaweed, and there would be his boat. Sometimes he wondered how he would get it off the bottom of the sea and up on top of the waves. Maybe the fairy would help with that, too.

So every day as Cletis fished for sponges, he also hunted for pretty and curious-shaped pieces of snowy white coral. Always he looked each piece over carefully and told himself: "This is a part of her robe. This is an elbow and this a lock of hair. This is a toe. See the nail?" He pretended he was asking his father, although he would never have dared actually to do so.

His mother's garden beds grew and grew. Thyme and other herbs and sweet-smelling flowers clambered over the little walks and terraces of coral. It was very pleasant and fragrant, and the family liked to sit there of an evening when the day's work had been done.

"This land is much like the islands of Greece," Cletis's father said to his mother one night.

"We have our grapes and our olives and our figs and lemons," his wife replied.

"I have my work and the sea is full of fish," he went on. "Soon I shall have a boat, too."

"We have our goats for milk and cheese, and our sheep for meat and wool."

"Best of all," her husband finished, "we have safety. That we did not have on Samos. Here, in this garden only love and peace dwell."

"It is the abode of good spirits," his wife murmured softly.

"Or fairies," her husband added.

Cletis looked at his father in amazement. Did he, too, want to believe in fairies? Did he, too, have desires that could not be filled in an ordinary man-made way? He had a home, and an orchard, and a vineyard, and sheep, and goats, and food, and clothing. Of course he wanted a boat; but everyone knew that!

Out there on the sea, when his father was alone with the wind and waves and sun and an occasional sea gull, what did he ask of this person or fairy he made up out of *his* own dreams to talk to?

As Cletis stared, his father leaned over and picked up a piece of coral.

"It looks like a hand," he said.

Cletis drew his lower lip between his teeth. He, too, had thought it looked like a hand. His father slipped his thick horny fingernail into a little crack and a flake of coral fell on his knee. He slid his nail along a ridge idly, and as he did so, other thin pieces of coral flaked off. He held the white lump up to the moonlight and peered at it carefully.

"Bring a candle," he said to Cletis. Then when he had flaked away every bit of loose coral with his thumbnail and the point of his knife, he laid a perfect white marble hand on his knee. Cletis and his father and mother stared at the hand in amazement.

News spread throughout Sfax, and for many days thereafter the men who fished for fish, and the men who fished for sponges, and their wives and children came to look at the marble hand. Sometimes the older folk teased Cletis a little, asking him what kind of fisherman he was. All the boys and girls were frankly envious of the attention he got. Cletis's mother put the hand on the mantel over the fireplace; and by and by, folks forgot about it.

Cletis did not, however. He liked to pretend that now he had found all of the pieces of his fairy whom the waves had broken to bits so many years ago. When he was in the room alone, he sometimes took hold of the tips of her marble fingers and talked to her. It was so easy to pretend, now that she was here.

"Thank you, Good Fairy, you are very kind," he said one day when he thought he was all alone. "I think more than anything else in all the world I should like a boat, a sponge boat, if you please."

"What would a little fellow like you do with a sponge boat?" a big voice boomed behind him.

Cletis spun around, and there in the doorway stood the biggest man he had ever seen. He was a head or more taller than Cletis's father. He wore queer clothes, too; and he was a little hard to understand when he talked. He reached over and unwound Cletis's fingers from the marble hand. When he held it up to the light, he drew his breath in sharply and exclaimed:

"Beautiful! Beautiful! Perfect! Greek work at least two thousand years old!"

Then he turned to Cletis.

"Are you the fellow who found this?" he asked.

Cletis nodded.

"Will you show me where? Will you go down with my divers and help them hunt for other pieces?" He kept on asking questions and Cletis kept on nodding.

Then the strange man explained to him that many hundreds of years ago very rich people lived in this part of Africa. They sent to Greece for beautiful things with which to make life pleasant. Later on, most of those things had gotten lost or destroyed, but sometimes pieces of statuary of beautifully carved marble were found. If Cletis could help him find more pieces, he would put them in a big museum where thousands of people could look at them and enjoy them.

"But to whom were you talking when I came in?" he asked. "To the hand? Why did you ask it for a sponge boat?"

Cletis couldn't help himself. Before he knew it he had told the stranger the whole story of the fairy he had made up so he would have someone to talk to down on the bottom of the sea among the sponge beds.

The strange man looked at the marble hand for a moment, then at Cletis. If the boy could have heard his thoughts, they would have sounded something like this: "Why not? Yes, why not? When I make a discovery, the whole civilized world rewards me. Why shouldn't this little fisherman have some reward, too?" But out loud he just said to Cletis—

"I don't look much like a fairy. Do I?"

"No," the little boy answered honestly.

"Six foot, two," the man said to no one in particular. "Two hundred twenty-five pounds, dressed in dusty khaki. Some fairy!" He threw back his head and laughed and laughed and laughed until he shook all over.

A few weeks later, a trim little boat anchored in the harbor of Sfax. On her prow was printed in big letters:

THE CLETIS

The next morning a happy boy and his father sailed out of the harbor.

"Where will the tuna be running today?" Cletis asked his father.

"Tuna? Who said anything about tuna?" his father demanded. "This is a sponge fisherman's boat!"

The Mariner's Rock

Miguel lived in the city of Tangier and his best friend was Tonio. Tonio was an old man who had no brother or sisters or wife or children—only a fishing boat. Every morning early, when the sun shone and the ocean was calm, Tonio unfurled the big white sail on his boat and put out to sea. There he stayed all day fishing unless a rainy squall or a bad wind drove him back into port.

Every morning Miguel was down at the dock to see Tonio put out to sea. And every evening he was there to see him come in again. How graceful the boat was with its sharp white triangle of canvas against the

blue sky and even bluer water! Sometimes the boat heeled over so far in tacking that waves washed over its deck and no one but Tonio could have kept it from upsetting altogether.

Tonio knew everything about the sea. He could tell the depth of the water under his boat by its color. He looked at a wave and knew whether the wind whipping its crest would make trouble for fishermen or not. He could locate fish when even the gulls failed. And he sailed farther out from land than any other captain. He could even look at a man and tell whether or not he would be handy with a boat.

Sometimes when a storm came up very suddenly, some of the fishing boats never came back. Miguel's father had been on such a boat. Since then, Miguel's mother had had to sew for rich women long hours every day to earn the bread she and her son ate. And Miguel longed for the time when he could work for Tonio on his boat and bring the money he earned to his mother. She said "No!" however, that Miguel had to work on land for a blacksmith or a merchant or a farmer just as soon as she could get the money to pay his apprentice fees and find a place for him. Tonio always looked Miguel's mother sharply in the face at those times, and then said, "No, of course, Miguel must work on land."

When that happened, Miguel would climb the hills back of Tangier and sit looking out to sea dreaming.

Tangier lies at the gateway to the Mediterranean Sea and is one of the sunniest cities in all the world. In northwest Africa, it lies right across the Strait of Gibraltar from Portugal. When Miguel climbed the hills back of Tangier, he could look across the Strait and on very clear days see the great Rock of Gibraltar.

When he climbed these hills he could also look down on Tangier and see how beautiful his home town really was. Only Miguel didn't call Tangier his home town although he had been born there and his father had been born there before him—and his great-great-great-grandfather!

He was not an African, he would have said. Not Miguel! No, sir! He was Portuguese. And his family was Portuguese. He had Tonio's word for that.

Sometimes Tonio climbed the hills with Miguel and sat in the sun looking out over the town at the Atlantic Ocean and told him wonderful tales of his people. A long, long time ago, Tonio said, they had been the greatest sailors on earth. They had hired Italians and Spaniards to build ships for them, the biggest ships the world had ever seen until then. Of course Miguel knew such ships wouldn't be much more than lifeboats for the huge steamers that slipped through the Straits of Gibraltar nowadays. But hundreds of years ago when Portuguese seamen brought such a ship into port, men came from all around the countryside to admire it and wonder at its great size. Why, sometimes such a boat was as much as sixty or even a hundred feet long.

And the sails on such a boat! "Spread of canvas," Miguel and Tonio called it. There were thirty or forty sails to each boat, and there were yards and yards of cloth in each sail. No tiny wisp of breeze could wander through that maze of sails without being caught and used to push the boat forward.

Up, up, up, straight and slender in the middle of each boat reared a mast. Only the strongest and best pines would do for a mast. Only a pine tree that had been buffeted by the wind, sleet and snow of a hundred mountain winters could possibly be strong enough. No captain dared risk the lives of his men on some weak, splintery stick of wood. A ship with a broken mast is at the mercy of the waves. Therefore, a ship that could not ride out a storm without the wind's snapping off its mast was as good as nothing.

Every voyage in those days was a year or more long. Straight out westward across the great Atlantic Ocean Miguel's forefathers had sailed. Out there to the west, far, far away, a new land had been discovered by an Italian. He had been laughed at by his own countrymen, and had had to go to the King and Queen of Spain for help. His name was Christopher Columbus. But he went only a little way, found a bit of land and then turned back. It was a

Portuguese (remember Magellan?) who first found
a way past that western land and sailed clear around
the earth. It was a very brave thing to do because at
that time everybody believed that if one went far
enough, he would come to the end of the earth and
just drop off into nothing!

Usually, however, the Portuguese sailors steered
southward, skirting the coast of Africa, all the way
down to the Cape of Good Hope on the southern-
most tip of South Africa. There was a rock there,
Tonio said, called the Mariner's Rock. Every old
Portuguese seaman felt himself in home waters until
he reached the Cape of Good Hope. From there on
eastward lay the great unknown—winds and currents
still uncharted; strange lands and stranger peoples;
wealth beyond any man's imagination; and sometimes
sickness and curious adventures. Of many things each
man wrote to his parents or his wife and children—or
his sweetheart!—and placed the letter under a certain
broad flat rock on the shore.

Any ship bound homeward with a cargo of silk
from China, hemp from India, pearls from Ceylon, or
cloves from Zanzibar, must pass the Mariner's Rock.
There was no other way home. And every ship
stopped at the Cape of Good Hope and its sailors
looked under the Mariner's Rock. They carried back
home with them the letters the men on the last out-
ward bound ship had placed there and left notes for

sailors on other vessels. That was the only way the letters were ever delivered for, of course, there were no postmen four hundred years ago!

More than anything else in all the world, Miguel wished he might have lived that many years ago and have sailed away to the far places of the earth with those brave men who were his ancestors. But since he didn't live four hundred years ago, but today, he wished for the next best thing—that his mother would let him join the crew of Tonio's fishing boat. But of course she always said, "No!" and after he had looked at her face for a second, Tonio, too, said, "No," that Miguel must work on shore.

But no merchant or blacksmith would take Miguel until his mother had paid the apprentice fees, and rich women paid so little for the sewing she did. After she and Miguel had bought a bite to eat each day, there was no money left. Sometimes Tonio gave them a nice fish and then she could save a few pennies. But just as soon as there was a dollar in her little hoard, Miguel's trousers fell to pieces and she had to buy him another pair.

One afternoon when Miguel lay stretched out on a level spot of ground high up above the town, wishing he were fishing with Tonio, he began to dream of the stories Tonio told him. He thought of those sailor boys long ago, saying good-bye to their mothers in Portugal and later leaving letters for them under the

Mariner's Rock. Sometimes such a letter might have been there only a day or two before it was picked up—sometimes it must have been weeks, or even months!

Miguel wondered what he would have written had he been on one of those boats. Of course there would have been a letter to his mother, and one to Tonio. Miguel picked up a plane tree leaf and smoothed it out on a flat rock. He then broke off a sharp pointed twig and scratched on the soft under-surface:

DEAR TONIO
I AM GOING TO CHINA
I HOPE YOU WILL GIVE
MOTHER A FISH NOW AND
THEN—SHE LIKES FISH BUT
SHE DON'T LIKE FISHERMEN
MIGUEL

The leaf was a big one, so Miguel scratched the out-lines of a sailing boat on one lobe and a basket of fish on another. He searched about him until he found a flat stone and tucked Tonio's letter well under it so the rain couldn't wet it, or the wind blow it away.

He would have to write his mother a much longer letter, of course, and he gathered several leaves. Miguel was not a very big boy, and it wasn't too easy to scratch so many letters on the plane tree leaves. It took a lot of time and energy, since it was the first time he had ever written letters to anyone. He didn't quite know what to say to his mother. She knew everything he did, and more, too. But he worked on and on, printing bits of the stories Tonio had told him about the Portuguese sailors of four hundred years ago.

He didn't notice that the sun was no longer shin-ing. It was only when the wind stole one of his leaves that he looked up and saw the black clouds scudding across the sky. There would be a storm and surely a bad one.

Miguel looked out to sea as the son of a fisherman always does when the sky darkens and the wind picks up leaves on land and little waves on the ocean. Far off on the horizon were a number of white dots. The storm had surprised the fishermen, too, and they were racing to get back to land before the waves grew too big. Miguel pinned the leaves of his mother's letter together with a thorn, and pushed it back under the rock with Tonio's and started down the path.

He hadn't taken more than a dozen steps, however, before he turned and hurried back. He looked about for a second, picked up a scrap of shale, and scratched on his crude post office:

MARINER'S ROCK

Before he finished big drops of rain dashed against his back, and in a moment he was drenched.

Miguel hurried down the path a second time. It was muddy and slick and dark. He couldn't see where to step and his feet slipped. Then it happened! One foot hit a loose rock, and when it turned over, Miguel sat down in the mud and started sliding. At first it was slowly and gently, but he couldn't stop himself or get up. Then it was faster and faster. He clutched at rocks but his hands were so muddy and they were so wet that his fingers slipped over the stones as though they weren't there. He clutched at weeds but they broke off in his hands or slipped out of the spongy earth, roots and all.

Miguel never knew where or when he slipped off the path. Any path in daylight, and when one is on one's feet, is quite a different matter from that same path, soupy with rain, under heavy dark clouds, and with night falling. It is a particularly different path when one is traveling on the seat of his trousers—or where the seat of his trousers used to be—and the small of his back. There was a big rock—and then Miguel went to sleep.

How long he slept, he didn't know, but when he awoke the stars were shining brightly overhead. Miguel stirred and then lay very still. After a moment he propped himself up on his elbows and looked at his feet. The right ankle was swollen. He started to move it cautiously, but stopped instantly for a sharp pain shot up his leg.

Miguel lay back on the ground and gazed up into the sky. When he was very quiet, he was not uncomfortable—except that his hip stung and itched a little from the ride over the pebbles on the path. He was not afraid. This close to the coast and the village of Tangier, there were no animals in the hills except for a little fox now and then. The foxes were pests, Miguel knew; they slipped into the vineyards at night and ate the grapes. But they were so afraid of human beings that it was hard to catch sight of one. Too, he knew that sooner or later when he did not return to his home, Tonio or his mother would come for him.

His foot hurt him a little and he turned over on his back so the leg could lie out straight. It felt easier that way. Up overhead the Great Dipper flared. Miguel's eyes turned instantly to the star at the end of its handle—the Pole Star by which all sailors steer their ships at night. That star had guided Miguel's father only a few years before—and his forefathers four hundred years ago when they sailed around the world in search of riches. It guided Tonio when dusk fell before he returned from fishing.

There was a murmur of voices and Miguel's heart beat with joy. Someone was coming for him! There was no other reason for anyone to be in the hills at night. The voices grew stronger and Miguel could see the glimmer of the flares they carried. The outlines of Tonio's face and shock of hair became distinct, and his mother's face framed in her dark shawl— and the faces and forms of neighbors.

After a few moments Miguel noticed that they were no longer coming toward him. They were passing! Then he knew he was not lying on the path but had fallen off it. He tried to call out, but it was like a dream. His lips and tongue formed the words but no sound came.

As his mother and her friends and neighbors passed up the path, Miguel started to cry. He dug his knuckles into his eyes, and his elbow hit a loose pebble. It rolled down the hillside and he could hear it bouncing about for a minute or more. He stopped crying, picked up another pebble and deliberately threw it down the hill. It made even more noise than the first.

Why hadn't he thought of that before? Miguel lay

flat on his back and began groping on both sides of himself for pebbles. Before the bobbing flares again appeared on the pathway with his mother's and Tonio's faces beneath them, he had a little pile of rocks beside him. Some were as big as his fist. They would make a good loud noise.

Again Miguel tried to call out and again his voice failed him. Lying there in the rain and cool night air had caused his throat to swell, he was pretty sure. When the little party of searchers were almost abreast of him, Miguel threw his first stone and then waited, watching the faces under the flares. It seemed ages before Tonio held up his hand for silence. Miguel threw another rock. Then another. And another.

"A little fox, maybe," someone in the group suggested.

Tonio said nothing, but holding his flare high above his head he plunged off the path toward the noise of falling stones. He almost stepped on Miguel.

"A little fox! Humph!" he sniffed. "No fox kicks stones down the hillside when a crowd of human beings is passing. A little boy, yes!"

He picked Miguel up and carried him home, then hurried off after the doctor who mends broken bones.

A warm bed and some good hot soup made from one of Tonio's fish soon took the soreness out of his throat. But Miguel lay in bed for days and then had to go about on crutches, his foot in a plaster cast.

It was fun to be the center of so much attention, but one thing worried Miguel. The doctor who mends broken bones costs a lot of money, and his mother earned so little. If only there were some way in which he could help! The day the doctor took the cast off his foot, Miguel spoke to Tonio about it.

"What?" Tonio almost shouted. "Do you mean to say you do not know? You are to fish with me on my boat."

"But my mother," Miguel whispered, "she will not let me. I am to be a farmer—or a blacksmith—or a merchant. As soon as she can save the money for the fees!"

"Pooh!" snorted Tonio scornfully. "A woman cannot earn enough to save money! It is you who must be the man of the family and earn enough to keep her so she does not have to sew from morning until night."

"I have told her so," Miguel cried, "but she will not let me. She is afraid of the sea because it took my father."

"She knows now that a sailor's son cannot dig in the soil or hammer iron or measure out ribbons and coffee for a living," Tonio said scornfully. "When she comes home tonight talk to her about it."

That evening Miguel hobbled about, saving his lame foot as much as he could, helping his mother prepare supper. The question— Might he go out in

Tonio's boat and became a fisherman?—was on the tip of his tongue a hundred times but he couldn't ask it. He was afraid. Always before the answer had been "No!" Every time he tried to speak the words, a lump came up in his throat and stuck there and it was impossible to get a sound past it.

But it was his mother herself who brought the matter up after supper was over and the kettle and spoons washed and put away. She opened a cupboard and took out a little bundle. Miguel waited breathlessly while she opened it and then stared. There was nothing but some dried plane leaves and a small, cheap medallion. She picked up a fragment of leaf and sighed.

"I knew that he, your father, loved the sea almost as much as he loved you and me," she said softly. "But I thought it was because he was used to it, because it was the only life he knew. So I decided that if I kept you away from it, you wouldn't love it as he did."

She was quiet for a moment and then went on, "Tonio is right. A sailor's son is born with the love of the sea in his heart."

She picked up a fragment of leaf and read: "Waves as high as the housetops are gentle billows to a Portuguese sailor."

"Pearls from Ceylon, silk from Japan, tea from China," she read from another fragment.

And "The sea is a surly slave that uncovers its

70

riches to brave men only," from a third.

"You—you found the letters under the Mariner's Rock?" Miguel whispered. "I told Tonio I was going to China, but I didn't mean it. I was only pretending."

"Yes, we found the Mariner's Rock, and Tonio knew there would surely be something under it. He knew you were pretending about China because no boat has sailed from Tangier for China for a long time."

"I wanted to write you, too, but I didn't know what to say," Miguel explained a little embarrassed. "I didn't know whether you would ever find the letter."

"Yes, I found it. But I discovered more than the letter," his mother answered. "I found out that because I am afraid of the sea, I was trying to make a coward of a brave man's son. Of the great-great-great grandson of the bravest sailors in the world! If a man is born with the roar of waves in his ears and the feel of a tiller in his hands, he can't listen all day to women haggling over the price of a yard of cloth."

She lifted the little gilt medallion, knotted a piece of strong cord through the link at the top and hung it about his neck.

"This is the medallion of Elmo, the patron saint of sailors. Your father wore it. Say a prayer to Saint Elmo when you put out to sea—and may God and he bring you safely back to me each evening."

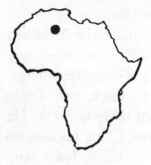

The First Lamb

His name was Abd el Karuzeh, and his father and mother pronounced it deep down in their throats so that each syllable sounded almost the same as all the others, like the echo of pebbles dropped into a deep well. It was a big name for a small boy, but his size was deceiving. He was older than he looked. None of the men and women who make their homes in the limestone caves in southern Algeria, in that low range of hills which separates the coastal plane from the desert, are big people.

Abd el Karuzeh was ten years old, and for two years now he had helped herd the village flocks. Every morning he and the other boys of his age went from cave to cave and called out the sheep and goats of the family or families living within. Then uphill they all trooped, following trails which only familiar eyes could recognize and scaling slopes which only sheep, goats, and boys bred to mountains could climb.

One by one, Abd el Karuzeh and the other boys rounded up out of the flock a dozen or so ewes with their lambs and stopped on some slope where the African sun had coaxed a faint tinge of green out of the jutting rocks and sour soil. Sheep were stupid creatures, Abd el Karuzeh's father said, and there had to be an abundance of food under their very noses—else they would starve to death! Farther on, where only weeds and thistles struggled against the rocks, the older boys pastured the goats. While beyond even that, among the crags where human eyes could discover almost no green thing, the boys were no longer children but not yet men, foraged along with the tribe's camels for a precarious existence. They did not return to the caves at night, but lived and slept with their grumbling, ungainly charges for months at a time. Therefore, each of them carried a spear, for no one knew when a lion would spring from a rock.

Abd el Karuzeh carried a dagger stuck through his belt, but lions seldom came close to the caves. He had only hyenas to fear—and then only after dark. Darkness comes quickly in the mountains once the sun has set. And well he knew that when shadows to the east of rocks began to grow blue, he must gather his ewes and their lambs together and hurry down the hill. The patter of hooves on the rocks was a dainty and light sound, but a hyena made no sound at all until its powerful jaws snapped through a lamb's neck.

The old men of the tribe said a hyena could follow a man unnoticed until its hot breath scorched his heels. There were evil spirits, Abd el Karuzeh had heard from these men, which lived among the rocks and roamed the hills at night. Sometimes they took the form of a hyena and followed travelers. Whenever one rose up onto its hind legs and whispered into a man's ear, that man spoke only foolishness from then on and became a burden to his tribe, said the old men.

But Abd el Karuzeh was not thinking of hyenas or foolish men one particularly sunny afternoon. He was swinging his bare legs over the edge of a huge rock and pitying himself a lot. His father was poor, to begin with. Poor, even for the cave dwellers of southern Algeria. He owned only a half dozen sheep, and he had not, like other fathers, given his son a lamb with which to start a flock of his own.

"You must earn your first lamb," he had replied shortly to Abd el Karuzeh's pleading. But he turned his face away when he said it, for Abd el Karuzeh's father loved his son and it was hard to deny him this thing.

74

Like all fathers he dreamed of the day when he would sit among the old men and listen to Abd el Karuzeh, then become a grown man, help direct the tribal council. But like all fathers he also knew that if Abd el Karuzeh did not own flocks of sheep and goats and camels, no one would listen to him. Poor men can be as good as rich men, but no one asks their advice. And how was any boy to start a flock without even one lamb to call his very own? So Abd el Karuzeh's father could not meet his son's eyes as he had replied, "You must earn your first lamb!"

So the boy sat perched on a big rock and dangled his legs down its warm sides as he wrestled with his problem. What could he do to earn a lamb? He asked himself the question a thousand times, but there was no answer. The only way Abd el Karuzeh had ever known a boy to get a lamb was for his father to give it to him. If his father was too poor—

Abd el Karuzeh did not like the thought. So he banged his bare calloused heels against the rock and squinted across the valley at the cliff ten miles away. He knew that above and below that cliff other boys were herding sheep and goats. Almost every one of those boys could look at his flock and point out a lamb, or perhaps a ewe and her lamb that belonged to him!

Abd el Karuzeh knew they loved their sheep. That when the anemones and cyclamen splashed color over the hills after the rainy season, they wove wreaths for

75

their sheep's necks and tied bouquets to their legs and fat tails. That of frosty nights when the fires died down and the heat had gone out of the caves, they crept among the animals in the corner and snuggled up to their own sheep for warmth.

But what could a boy do to earn a lamb? Even a sickly lamb? Or a crippled lamb? If he could kill a lion or a leopard and bring the skin to the Headman, then the tribe would give him almost anything—a sheep, a goat, even a camel! But Abd el Karuzeh knew that not many grown men had killed a leopard, and even fewer had killed a lion. No, he would have to think of some other way.

What could he do? And when could he do it? He arose every morning before the sun had cleared all of the mist away from the cave entrance, took the bit of bread and cheese his mother gave him, and set off for the hills with the other shepherds. There he kept one eye out for eagles which might carry off a lamb that had strayed too far from its mother, and watched with the other for any small anmial he might kill with a rock and roast over a little fire of thorns for his mid-day meal.

A shout aroused Abd el Karuzeh and he looked up to greet another shepherd. The sun was already red in the western sky and the shepherds were rounding up their flocks to return to the caves. Abd el Karuzeh, being one of the youngest boys, did not go so far into the hills as the others, so he waited as they brought up their sheep. The sun sank lower and lower, and the crags to the west pierced its red disk.

"Fuad and Feragi are late," one shepherd murmured uneasily, looking at the blue shadows already stealing across the lowest rocks.

"Do you see them anywhere, Abd el Karuzeh?" asked another. "Your eyes are sharp."

Abd el Karuzeh scanned the slopes, but there was no sign of the two boys and their flock. The uneasiness among the boys grew. Fuad and Feragi were brothers and sons of the Headman, but the boys would have waited for their poorest comrade. No shepherd deserts a fellow shepherd in the hills at night. For the hyena, which is a skulking coward under the sun, is feared by grown men under the stars. Where were Fuad and Feragi? Even the sheep and goats bunched together as though afraid.

But what was that? It sounded like the patter of raindrops on dry leaves. A sigh of relief broke from the boys and even the flock started milling about as though glad. Hurrying down the pathway came the Headman's sons and their sheep. But they were not happy boys.

"We have had to abandon a lamb," said Fuad, the elder of the two.

Relief among the boys changed to dismay. Not

only are his charges wealth to a shepherd; he loves them as a mother loves the baby that depends upon her helplessly. And just as no mother will desert her baby, neither will a good shepherd desert one of his flock.

"What happened?" someone asked in a low voice, and every boy strained forward listening.

Feragi pointed to a big white ewe that kept sniffing the lambs of the flock and bleating softly now and then. She was hunting for a lamb which was not there!

"She-of-the-Nimble-Toes strayed off a bit from the flock," he said, "and I went after her to bring her back. When I was but several steps from her, I saw an adder among the stones between us, and I threw a rock at it. I crushed the poisonous snake's head, but our ewe, She-of-the-Nimble-Toes, was frightened and leaped sideways, knocking her lamb over the cliff."

"Could you not reach it?" Abd el Karuzeh knew the answer before he asked.

"No," Fuad replied. "It fell on a small ledge and if we could have gotten down to it, we could not have climbed back up again. It is a pity, too, for She-of-the-Nimble-Toes comes of good stock, and her lambs make fine sheep."

"And it was unhurt," Feragi put in.

"It will not remain unhurt long," Fuad remarked

shortly. "Even now a hyena or the jackals may have it. Oh, we tried to get it, of course, but the rock was brittle and snapped under our hands, and the bushes broke under our weight. We were each too big and heavy."

"I thought Fuad was going to fall once," Feragi interrupted.

"And you dangled your cloak over the cliff for me to hold on to—and risked being pulled over after me. Didn't you? You are a brave, good brother!"

"I'd rather have you than a lamb any day," Feragi grinned, although he was embarrassed by his brother's praise.

"Well, you have me. But it is late and we must get the rest of the flock back to the caves before we lose any more," Fuad replied as he started his companions and the animals down the trail.

A lamb, a fine lamb, alive and unhurt on a ledge where a boy might reach it! It seemed wicked to Abd el Karuzeh to abandon it to wild animals.

"Yah hya ris!"

The shepherds were singing as they always did on the way home at night, one boy carrying the melody and the others joining in on the chorus in a sad minor key:

"Yah hya ris!" Yes, my Captain!

They did not notice that Abd el Karuzeh had fallen behind them. He stopped short. Back there in the gathering darkness was a lamb, a good lamb, alive, unhurt—on a ledge where he might rescue it. Back there, too, there might be jackals or hyenas ready to devour either lamb or boy!

"Yah hya ris!" came the chorus of the shepherds' song. That way lay food, fires, companionship, safety. As Abd el Karuzeh looked after the boys, he saw Fuad stride over to a tired lamb, pick it up, and swing its soft body around his neck like a collar. Fuad was a good shepherd. He would never have deserted a lamb if it had been at all possible for him to rescue it.

With sudden determination, Abd el Karuzeh turned and trotted off into the darkness. One by one the stars pierced the Algerian sky and the moon swam in a faint azure glow.

"Yah hya ris!"

Abd el Karuzeh found himself singing under his breath as he hurried along. When he thought of the words of the song he could not think of what might lurk in the shadows. And when he sang, even faintly, he could not hear what might creep up behind him.

A stone rolled down the hillside and he began to run in terror. Was there really anything following him? He clasped his hands over his ears so he could hear no evil. He had no desire to go through life talking foolishness! On and on he sped, his heart in his throat and his pulse pounding in his ears.

His foot dashed another stone downhill and his

pulse struck a new note. Or was it his pulse? He jerked his hands from his ears and listened.

Baaaaaaah!

Only a lamb—a cold lamb—bleated like that!

Ba-a-a-a-a-a-a-h!

He followed the quavering sound. Here was the cliff. Here was a clean space where Fuad's and Feragi's bodies had brushed all the dirt and stones aside as they had tried to worm their way down the cliff. And there, looking up at him from below, was She-of-the-Nimble-Toes' lamb!

Abd el Karuzeh took off his cloak, slid on his stomach over the cliff, and with his toes felt for a bit of jutting rock. Almost inch by inch the boy descended, his body plastered to the rock in front of him, his skin wet with sweat from exertion and the nervous strain. Time after time as he eased his weight from one foot to the other the rock crumbled and went crashing down the mountain side. Only his strong fingers saved him. Fuad had been right. The shrubs were too small and the rock too brittle and crumbly to have held a larger boy.

At last he stood on the ledge beside the lamb. He picked it up and it nuzzled its head against his chest. As he stroked its warm wool, he could see in the pale moonlight that there were stains on its back and he saw, too, that his fingers were bleeding.

Blood has a very strong odor to animals. Abd el

Karuzeh cowered back against the cliff and peered to the right and left of him. There was no time to waste. The smell of blood would surely bring animals, and quickly. He slung the lamb about his neck as he had seen Fuad do, took off his belt, and tied its feet together.

Climbing down the cliff had been slow, hard work. Climbing up was even slower and more difficult. He was tired. His fingers hurt. The lamb about his neck made him feel awkward and off balance. Its feet scraped the rock. He could not plaster his face as close to the cliff as he wanted to—as he knew was safe! If the lamb grew nervous and kicked, even a little bit, it might plunge them both into the abyss below. There might be a hyena jumping for his feet—or one waiting for him above. His pulse pounded in his ears so loudly he could hear nothing.

It seemed an eternity before his hands had struck a broad expanse of level rock and he had wormed his thin little belly back over the top of the cliff. To safety?

Abd el Karuzeh was not quite sure how far he was from his father's cave. He looked down the long pathway he must cover and his breath caught in his throat. A gleam of light! Was it a hyena's eyes? Now many gleams! A pack of jackals?

Then he laughed aloud—animals' eyes are in pairs, and they are steady in the darkness. These lights bobbed up and down singly. Too, animals tread softly, and Abd el Karuzeh's keen ears caught the sound of footsteps almost as soon as he had seen the torches.

"Säiida," he shouted, pulling the second syllable out into a long high-pitched note: e-e-e-e-e-e-e-e!

"Säii (e-e-e-e-e-e-e-) da!" "Hallo-o-o-o-o-o-o-o!" came back his father's voice before his own echoes had died away. The rocks rattled beneath his feet as he sped down the path; but there was no need to slip along quietly now. No animal, however hungry or fierce, attacks a party of men with fire in their hands.

Fuad and Feragi were in the group, and their father. Abd el Karuzeh untied the lamb and placed it in Fuad's hands.

"Why do you do that, Abd el Karuzeh?" the Headman asked.

"Did not your sons tell you?" Abd el Karuzeh asked in surprise. "It belongs to you. It is the lamb of your ewe, the one we shepherds call She-of-the-Nimble-Toes."

"It is a lamb my sons abandoned to die," the Headman replied slowly, "therefore, it no longer belongs to anyone in my family. We could not wear its wool with satisfaction. We could not eat its flesh with pleasure. When it is grown, we could not claim its lambs with honor.

"Fuad," the Headman turned to his son, "return

the lamb to its rightful owner!"

Tears slid from Abd el Karuzeh's eyes and sank into the lamb's soft wool. It was not manly to cry, he knew; but now not only his fingers throbbed—but his heart was very full.

"Abd el Karuzeh!" His father spoke sharply as poor men the world over are apt to do when they are very proud of their children. The boy sank on one knee before the Headman and laid his forehead upon the palm of the Headman's hand in sign of thanks and tribal submission.

Then, with Fuad on one side and Feragi on the other, and his lamb—*his very own lamb*—cradled in his arms, Abd el Karuzeh followed the men back to the safety, warmth, and companionship of the caves.

Katya Wanted a
Room of Her Own

Katya lived in a house with eighteen other people. There was Grandfather and Grandmother, Father and Mother and baby brother, besides two uncles and their wives and seven children, and un unmarried uncle and aunt. Naturally it was a big house; but even so, it rather overflowed, especially when Katya's two married aunts came home for a visit and brought their children with them!

Not that Katya felt that the house was especially crowded. *Boers*, as Afrikaners are sometimes called, always had large families, and the children usually stayed at home. The custom was that when a young man married, he brought his wife home with him. It was then, when the grandchildren came along, that the old homestead had a way of overflowing.

In many ways this arrangement saved a lot of bother and trouble. When a young man got married he didn't have to build a new house or buy new furniture. Sometimes when a family was really large —more than a mere nineteen people—the grandfather, who was always the head of the household, and his sons and grandsons would build an additional two or three rooms onto the house. A common pastime for the men during the long rainy seasons, was to carve beautifully grained wooden boards for the tops of chests and the fronts of clothespresses and cupboards. A Boer farmer would consider it unforgivable extravagance to spend good money at a store for tables and chairs and chests that could be made at home, and made much stronger and better, too.

No one in Katya's family spent much time visiting because, with the exception of the daughters who grew up and married neighbor boys and went to their homes to live, all of the relatives were right under one roof. Neither were there many letters to write. One of Katya's unmarried uncles was going to school in Capetown, however. He was studying animal husbandry. Grandfather usually announced at the supper table when he was going to write the college student, who was Katya's Uncle Jan. Everyone

joined in telling Grandfather what to say, making the letters a family affair.

"Please ask Uncle Jan to send me more books," Katya always begged.

Then Grandmother would look over her small iron-rimmed spectacles at Katya. Now Grandmother had never learned to read, but she could darn a stocking faster and more neatly than any of her daughters or daughters-in-law or grandchildren. Katya could darn a stocking very neatly, but she liked to hide a book in her darning basket and read several chapters while she was supposed to be working.

Naturally, in a household where there are nineteen people, it would be hard to do a thing like this without being found out. As a result, Katya often had to dry all the dishes by herself without any help. Or maybe she would have to make all the beds in the children's room alone—as punishment.

Because she always got caught when she was reading instead of doing her work, Katya began to wish for something mentioned often in her books—a room all by herself. Sometimes the stories in the books Uncle Jan sent were about England and even far-away America.

According to the stories, in those countries every girl seemed to have a room all her own, and as far as Katya could tell, she didn't have to share anything in it with anybody else. That meant that if there were a dresser, she could use all the drawers. She didn't have to crowd everything she owned into one corner to make room for a half dozen other children. Nor would she have to hang all her dresses and aprons on one or two pegs in the closet either. Katya sometimes opened the closet in the children's room and wondered how it would look with only her five or six dresses and five or six aprons hanging there. They would look lost, she had to admit!

Katya wondered if a girl who had a room all by herself ever got lonely in the middle of the night. Whom did she snuggle up to when it was cold? Katya loved to get in bed with Cousin Ellen on cold nights. Cousin Ellen was plump, and her feet were always warm.

Suppose a girl sleeping all by herself had eaten too many dumplings for supper? Or too much apple strudel? Who would fix a hot-water bottle for her tummy? Suppose she got a toothache and the whole side of her face throbbed and throbbed with sharp pain? Even when no one could do anything for the tooth, it helped a lot, of course, just to know that Cousin Ellen was there and was sorry.

But Katya didn't spend much time thinking about what might happen in the middle of the night. What bothered her was that it was the middle of the morning and the middle of the afternoon when she was interrupted every time she got deep in the most exciting part of a story. Now a girl who had a room all by herself could read and read and read, when the morning and midday chores were over. She could probably read all the books in the world!

Of course, Katya didn't spend all her time darning stockings and reading and wishing for a room all by herself. She could cook and clean and knit socks, and had lots of these things to do. She also knew how to garden and how to care for the poultry. Her grandfather always pruned the fruit trees and the grape vines himself, and he said he would rather have just Katya help him than the boys.

Sometimes when Katya and Grandfather worked together, she told him stories she had read of girls like herself in England and America. Sometimes he told her stories of his own childhood in Holland. His father, Katya's great-grandfather, had been a teacher at the University of Amsterdam. There had been lots of children in that home, too. Lots of children and lots of books! As a child, Katya's grandfather had read many stories, and she could tell that he didn't think it was such a terrible thing for a girl to be reading a book when she should be darning a stocking.

Because he did not consider the little one-roomed school which all the children in the community attended a very good one, Grandfather had sent most of his sons to school in Capetown. Some of his sons had even gone to college—like Uncle Jan, for instance. His daughters, however, had attended the little one-roomed country school. Grandmother did not think book learning so very necessary for a girl. She thought the ability to cook and manage a house and darn a socking of much greater importance, and she did not hesitate to say so.

Now one evening when the family was still at the supper table, after Grandfather had read aloud a letter of Uncle Jan, he turned to Katya.

"How would you like to go to Capetown and go to school there?" he asked.

Katya's father and mother sat perfectly quiet. Perhaps the question didn't surprise them so much! The old grandmother sniffed loudly and started to say something but changed her mind. Grandfather had a way of looking at his grandchildren which meant he didn't intend to have any back talk, and he was looking at Grandmother the very same way now!

Katya didn't know what to reply. If she said, "Yes," Grandmother wouldn't like it. If she said, "No," Grandfather wouldn't like it. She didn't have any idea whether her father and mother would be happy or sorry. In fact, she didn't know what she herself wanted. So she only smiled shyly at Grandfather, and he smiled back in a way that made his mustache look like a brush at the corners.

"Oh, Cousin Katya," Cousin Ellen whispered delightedly, on the way up to bed after the dishes were done and Grandfather had read from the big Bible bound in cowhide, "wouldn't it be wonderful if Grandfather should send you to school in Capetown? He has never sent one of his daughters or granddaughters away to school before!"

"He didn't say he was going to send me," Katya replied.

"Silly," Cousin Ellen nodded, "I believe he has his mind already made up. You know as well as anything that Grandfather doesn't talk just to make a noise!"

Katya knew that Cousin Ellen was right.

Nothing much more was said in the family about Katya's going away to school in Capetown—at least before Katya—but it was taken for granted that the next time Uncle Jan came home on vacation he would take her back with him. All the aunts sewed for Katya, and it wasn't long before she had a pile of underwear, frocks, and aprons higher than she was tall.

Grandmother went over Katya's manners as though she expected to find some hidden habit of rudeness. This went on and on until Katya began answering, "Yes, Grandmother," and "No, Grandmother," like a little mechanical doll.

At last everything was ready and Uncle Jan came home. He had a few days vacation, and it seemed to Katya the morning would never come when they would drive off to the station where she and Uncle Jan were to take the train for Capetown. It did, however, and everybody kissed Katya good-bye and shook hands with Uncle Jan—everybody, that is, but Grandmother. She kissed him, too, and said to him "You must visit your niece, Katya, at least once a week and see that she minds her manners!"

Katya had never been on a train before, and it was a wonderful experience. Trees, fields, telegraph poles all rushed past at an astonishing rate. Even villages popped out of nowhere and rapidly shrank in the distance behind them. Uncle Jan had all he could do to keep Katya from hanging out of the window so far that she was in danger of being scraped away by a tree or bridge.

Katya's golden pigtails and her shy sweet smile won the hearts of the other passengers in their compartment on the train. When she remarked to Uncle Jan that the small compartment—or room on the train—was as full of people as her bedroom at home was full of cousins, a little old lady asked her what she expected to find at school.

"I'm going to have a room all by myself so I can read, *and read, and READ* all I want to," Katya replied.

"O-o-o-o-o-o-oh!" The little old lady drew the word out as though she hated to let go of it, and nodded her head vigorously at the same time.

"Uncle Jan has a room all by himself," Katya explained proudly.

"Are you going to the same school as your uncle?" the old lady asked.

It was Katya's turn to say, "No-o-o-o-o-o-o!"

"Things might be a little different at your school, you know," the little old lady suggested, and smiled at Uncle Jan. But Katya was quite sure everything would be all right.

It was early evening when the train pulled into the Capetown station, and very dark by the time. Uncle Jan and Katya and a big strong man carrying Katya's box, reached the girls' school she was to attend. The headmistress was a tall woman, and Katya had to crick her neck back to see her face. Uncle Jan talked to the headmistress a few minutes, gave her some money, and signed some papers. Then he patted Katya's shoulder awkwardly, saying, "Now mind your manners," and went away.

There were only Katya and the headmistress in the room when Uncle Jan left. It was not a big room, but it seemed terribly empty with only two people in it—and one of them a stranger! The headmistress rang a bell and another tall woman appeared. Katya had to tilt her head back to look in this woman's face, too, and she began to wish for someone whose eyes were on a level with her own. This second teacher would take Katya to her room and help her unpack and arrange her clothes, the headmistress said.

Katya remembered her manners and held the door open for this other teacher. The halls were big and bare and quiet, and Katya's footsteps clattered. She walked on her tiptoes to kill the noise. Katya wished Cousin Ellen were with her. Cousin Ellen was always such a comfort.

Then the teacher opened a door and motioned Katya to enter. She saw a good-sized room with eight white beds in two prim rows. At the head of each was a small table, and at the foot a small wooden chest. There were pictures on the walls and books and lamps on the tables. One or two had little bouquets of flowers. It was the first spot in the school Katya had seen that didn't look big and bare and terribly empty.

"This is your bed. And these are your table and chest," the teacher was saying.

"There are seven other girls here?" Katya asked.

"Yes," the teacher replied. "We used to have all of the girls sleep in one great big dormitory. But now we put them in smaller rooms like this—seven girls to each room, and one older girl to look after them and take care of them whenever they need anything."

One older girl! Maybe she'd be a bit like Cousin Ellen! Maybe if you ate too many dumplings or too much strudel for supper, this older girl would get a hot-water bottle for your tummy. Maybe, when you had a toothache, she would let you creep into bed with her.

"You'll like the girls," the teacher smiled, "they are all jolly and nice."

"I thought—" Katya began. "I—I—was afraid I'd have a room all by myself." She hesitated a moment and then went on, "That would be terribly lonely, wouldn't it?"

"Oh, we wouldn't think of putting a girl all by herself," the teacher answered. "We want you to be happy here, and to learn as much as you can. And learning to live and work and play with other girls is just as important as anything you will ever get from books, you know."

A bell tinkled in the hall outside.

"Now brush your hair and put on a clean apron," the teacher told Katya, "and we'll go down to supper. You'll see all of the other girls in the dining room."

As they turned to go out, Katya murmured so softly the teacher scarcely heard her: "I'm glad I don't have to be all by myself. I don't think I'd like that!"

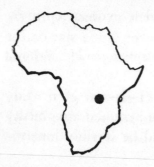

The Okapi Belt

Sleetan has never seen bright sunlight. This may sound queer to you for he was born and had lived all of his life on the equator where, as everyone knows, the sun beats down fiercely every day of the year. However, Sleetan lived deep in the great jungles of the Congo, and the only treeless strips of land he had ever seen were the narrow paths used by the forest animals and his own tribesmen. High overhead the boughs of giant forest trees tangled with long, strong vines to form a green canopy. Vines, trees, and bushes shut out every hint of direct sunlight. Sleetan lived by day in a cool green twilight, and by night in inky darkness. He went to sleep with the birds, and it is doubtful if he ever saw a star or the moon shining through that dark canopy of trees and vines.

He had looked up the tall straight trunks of many trees, but he had never seen a tree standing all by itself, trunk, branches, and topmost shoot, out in the sunlight.

The sides of Sleetan's home, which you might not even call a home, were made of bark stripped from tree trunks, and the roof was merely leafy branches laid across sticks. There was no need to build a better home for Sleetan's father and mother never stayed in one spot more than three or four days—and besides, it was never cold! In fact, Sleetan was ten years old, but he had never worn a stitch of clothing in his life except the rope of bark fibers over one shoulder and under the other arm which held a quiver of arrows slantwise across his back.

Sleetan's father wore a belt made of okapi skin. Okapi skin belts were important, for okapi skin was a badge of manhood—something like long trousers and shaving.

Sometimes, but these occasions were rare, Sleetan's father, or one of the other men of the tribe, came hurrying into camp to say that the hunters had killed an okapi. Then everyone left his little brush and bark shelter, and moved to the spot where the dead okapi lay and made a new camp. This was much simpler than one might think, for no man in the tribe owned anything but the pair of little bark aprons he wore, his okapi skin belt and his weapons. It was much simpler to move the tribe than it was to move a dead animal!

Especially was this true when the animal was an okapi, the largest of the deep jungle creatures. The top of Sleetan's head would come just about to an okapi's knees; and his father might stand upright under an okapi's stomach, that is, if an okapi would ever let him! Of course, that was because Sleetan and his father and mother belonged to a tribe of Pygmies who were never more than four feet tall.

Even so, the okapi was a big animal, almost as tall as a giraffe. It was so shy that men could seldom get close to one. It could stand so still and its legs were so crisscrossed with light and dark markings like trunks of saplings that a Pygmy could pass within a few feet of one and not know it was there. It was clever enough to hide its calf away so that even the best tracker in the tribe could not find it. It was so strong that it could break a good-sized sapling in two with one bunt from its bony head. Or, that failing, it could whirl about and smash a trunk as large as its knee joint with one kick from its hoof. Lastly, it was absolutely fearless and when cornered would charge any number of men. When that happened, there was always great sorrow in the tribe, for then at least one man met his death. Sleetan's father said that whoever ate enough okapi meat would undoubtedly become brave and clever and strong like the okapi. Whoever wore a belt of okapi skin would surely command the respect of the other jungle animals and birds and snakes. No one man could ever kill an okapi by himself; therefore, the skin always belonged to the tribe. A council of the oldest men cut the hide up into lengths suitable for belts and decided who among the tribe most deserved them. Whenever Sleetan looked at his father's okapi belt, he hoped that some day he, too, would deserve one. He knew he would never inherit his father's, for when his father died, it would be buried with him.

Sleetan's father made him a blow gun and taught him how to make his own darts. The boy practiced by the hour, shooting at a toadstool or a bit of lichen on an old log so he would neither lose nor break his darts. It was not long before the boy could puff up his cheeks, like a squirrel with a mouthful of nuts, and pop a leaf from its stem far over his head.

Older hunters carried little bags of poison. A pinch of that on a dart and the small animal whose hide it pierced would die within a few seconds. No more than three or four darts were needed to kill the feared and coveted okapi. So quickly did this poison kill an animal that it did not spread through the body. When a little bit had been cut away from around the wound, the rest of the flesh was used as food.

One day Sleetan's father had been standing on the banks of the Great River that flowed into the west. He came back to the tribe and said, "I have seen three full-grown okapis standing on the opposite shore!"

This river was so broad that the tribe had never tried to build one of its hanging bridges across it. But three okapis all at once! The next day every hunter in the tribe hid in the trees along the banks and silently waited. Along in the afternoon several okapis came down to the opposite shore to drink. And the next day it was the same! Across that broad and turbulent river there was plenty of meat. Good fine okapi meat! But how could they ever reach that other bank? Half of the tribe went upstream, half journeyed downstream, both searching for a narrower channel where a hanging bridge of vines could be slung. Many days passed before anyone reported the least success. Even then, the old ones doubted if the only possible place found were narrow enough.

Now everyone set to work cutting long slender vines, big vines to use as cables, little vines for ropes. The boys borrowed the men's hunting knives, cut down hundreds of saplings and trimmed them smooth and chopped them into even lengths. The young men climbed the tallest trees and examined their branches until they found a limb that was high enough, big enough, sound enough and far enough out over the river.

Then they fastened a good long vine to the branch, and one of the men got ready to swing across the river. Before he leaped out of the tree on which he was standing, he must hold fast to the vine and high enough so he would not hit the water. If he did hit the water, his bones might be broken. Or he might be jerked loose and swept away with the current.

The oldest men most skilled in bridge building squinted this way and that, measuring heights and distances and lengths in their minds. At last when they had chosen a spot on the vine, a tribesman grasped it at that exact place, and gave a mighty leap, shoving his body as far out as he could.

Down! Down! Down he swung, clearing the water by about two heights of a man. But now up! Up! Up in a great lazy arc the man on the vine swung. And then down, down, down, and up, up, up again onto the branch from which he had jumped came this human pendulum.

"I missed the opposite tree by two lenghths of a man," he said. "Perhaps if I hold a little lower on the vine I can reach out and grasp the twigs on the other side. I can curl my body up in a ball when I am over the water."

It was a brave thing for him to offer, but it was for the good of the tribe, and they accepted it in silence which he knew meant respect. Again he swung—down! Down! Down! And up! Up! Up! And then down! Down! Down! Down! And up! Up! Up! Back onto the same limb on the same side of the river. This time he made no remark to the tribe but grasped the vine a little lower, and, before anyone could protest, swung out over the river again.

"It's no use," he spoke sadly, at last, from his perch on the limb. "My nostrils caught the spray of the rapids—but my fingers only brushed the slenderest twigs." He opened his clenched hand and bits of torn leaves floated to the ground. This plan had failed.

That evening Sleetan found it difficult to sleep. He could not get the long vine, hanging motionless now, out of his mind. In the haze between sleeping and waking it reminded him of a snake dangling from the branch. A long slender body wrapped around a limb with the equally long tail dangling. Sometimes that tail wrapped itself around an unwary animal or a careless Pygmy. A long tail wrapped around a boy! Why not a long vine wrapped around a boy? Sleetan chuckled deep down in his throat. He had the answer!

The next morning Sleetan told his father. He would wrap the vine around his own body up to the point the old men had considered safe at first. Then he would hold on with both hands until he was across the river. On the upswing he would let go and unroll his body to the end of the vine. If that were tied around his waist, he would have both hands free with which to grasp the branches opposite.

Sleetan's father called the old men together and told them of his son's idea. They listened carefully. Finally one spoke. "It is an old man's thought in a child's body," he said.

A dozen young men leaped forward. "Sleetan is a child. This calls for strength. Let me do it!"

"Let me!"

"Let!"

"Choose me!"

"Do you understand the risk?" another old man asked the eager youths. "If you let go of the vine entirely and unroll too fast, the jerk when you come to the end may injure you badly. If you unroll to the full length of the vine and do not catch onto the tree opposite or do not get a good hold and are torn loose, you will be dashed into the rapids below."

"I would try it!"

"And I!"

"And I!"

Sleetan choked down a sob. It had never occurred to him either last night or this morning when talking to his father but that he would be the one to try out his scheme. But he was only a small boy, no taller than an okapi's knee; and of course it would not be proper for him to voice his disappointment, much less question a decision of the old men. He watched his father and the other men fasten the vine around the lucky young man's waist and wind him up in it.

The young man drew a deep breath and leaped. Down! Down! Down he swept. Even the birds were quiet. Every eye strained as they saw his hands loosen their grip on the vine when he began the upswing. Slowly, slowly he let his body unroll and then held out his hands to grasp the branches among which he was dashed. For a second he was lost to sight. Leaves came fluttering down. The outer twigs quivered.

Was his grasp secure? Was he uninjured? Or would he fall? The long vine, swinging in an arc high over the rapids, began swaying up and down and a shout of joy arose from the tribe on the bank. He was safe! He was tying the vine, the first cable on their bridge, to the trunk of the tree.

In a few minutes they heard the young man shout that he had finished his work. Then Sleetan's father tied a vine around his waist and started across on the first vine—hand over hand, high above the river. Another man followed him. And another! And another! By early afternoon a frail-looking but really strong bridge swayed between the two giant trees on opposite sides of the bank. The whole tribe—old men, warriors, women, and children—crossed the river.

That night they slept near the bridge. Early the

next morning the young men and warriors went down the river in search of okapi. It was not long before word came that there had been a kill, and the women and children moved on.

When they came up to the warriors, Sleetan noticed that although the okapi had been skinned, no belts had been cut out of its hide. Sleetan eyed it with longing. Every Congo Pygmy boy eyes an okapi skin with longing, as the sign of manhood—the badge of merit awarded by the old men of the tribe. The wise ones would burn a skin, precious as it is, rather than have a scrap of it fall into unworthy hands. Sleetan wondered who would receive belts cut from this hide. Undoubtedly the young man who had risked his life swinging across the river. He had done a good job and deserved honor.

Then the chief took his knife and began cutting out a belt. This was always a tense moment for the men and boys, and everyone watched carefully. Sleetan caught his lip between his teeth. The chief's knife had slipped. The strip he had cut off was too short. It would never go around a man. He was embarrassed for the chief and glanced at him pityingly.

But the chief was looking at Sleetan and smiling. As the young man had done! As they were all doing!

The chief fastened the belt around Sleetan and then made a little speech to him and to the tribe. Sleetan could not be just sure what he said. It was something about wise thoughts in a youthful body, and strength and bravery being good things but not enough. Sleetan was not quite sure what he said or what he meant. His heart beat too hard, and his pulse pounded in his ears. He clenched his hands into little hard fists so he could not finger his okapi belt while the chief was speaking. And he held his body so straight he must surely have reached at least half an inch above a full-grown okapi's knee.

Melanie

Melanie lived in a big palace. It was such a big palace that no one lived in most of it nowadays. Melanie's father, the King of Zanzibar—an island off the East Coast of Africa—was not one-hundredth as rich as his father, Melanie's grandfather, had been. Nor did he hold the power of life and death over all his subjects as Grandfather once did. In those days every room in the palace had been crowded, for hundreds of relatives and soldiers and servants had lived in the spacious rooms.

Now Melanie and her father—who had many servants and plenty of money, nevertheless—and her mother and brother lived in just a few beautiful rooms in the palace, furnished with carved benches and tables, with soft mats on the floor. Sometimes very rich and important men came to visit Melanie's father, and then they were entertained in some still more beautiful rooms with soft rich carpets, silk hangings and stained glass windows.

The change occurred within the palace after the day the big gunboat had sailed into the narrow strip of water separating the island of Zanzibar from Africa. Melanie's father—who was only a little boy then—could still remember the many soldiers in bright uniforms who came ashore. The leader of the soldiers spoke to the little boy's father, Melanie's grandfather. What he said was something like this.

"You have a choice of two things. Let us make your laws and collect the taxes from your people. If you do this, we'll pay you a goodly sum of money each year and the people will still call you King. But if you do not want to do this, we'll use our cannons to destroy your palace and kill your people."

Now, though Melanie's grandfather had plenty of soldiers, he didn't have any cannons. Too, some of his guns were a little rusty. So he took the first choice —and a good choice it was, for he lived very comfortably without any troubles or anything to worry about for the rest of his life. The foreign soldiers did most of the work and all of the worrying and paid him a sum of money regularly each year.

Of course he didn't need a big army any more, nor nearly so many servants, and gradually the relatives left the palace and went somewhere else to live. So little by little a great many of the rooms in the huge palace emptied, and people gradually forgot which uncle or cousin or captain had lived in each. The windows blew out and the doors blew off and the sun and rain cracked and peeled the plaster on the walls. But since no one had any use for them, these rooms were not repaired.

When Melanie's grandfather died, his son became king under the foreign soldiers. Everything was the same as it had been before except that the soldiers did not pay the new king quite so much money as they had the old king. They said he had never been used to quite so much, and therefore didn't need it. Also the foreign soldiers ate more than the native soldiers had, and it cost more to support them. Still, the new king, Melanie's father, had all the money he needed, and didn't have to worry about much of anything—so he was pretty well off.

The palace was built like one great huge square—something like the sides of a hollow box—and inside was a garden much larger than a poor man's farm. In it were palm trees and sweet-scented lemon trees, orange trees bearing both golden fruit and snowy blossoms at the same time, and many other trees and shrubs useful for their fruits and beautiful for men to look at.

In the garden were countless flowers of all kinds— from huge orchids which clung to the branches of old trees far over Melanie's head, and roses and geraniums and pinks, down to sweet English violets. And, oh! many others. Like the house, there were parts of the garden that weren't used or cared for any longer. Only instead of going to wrack and ruin as the house did, the garden just grew greener and richer and thicker where no one cut it back. Things grow like that in those parts of Africa where the sun is hot and where there is plenty of rainfall. In some places the bushes were so thick that Melanie couldn't force her way through them. There were always flowers blooming and birds singing in the trees all the year round.

It was a good thing that the garden and the rooms of the palace in which the family lived were so pleasant, for the only windows were in the outer walls and they were very small and very high up. Melanie was never permitted near the big front door, so she had never seen the world outside of her home. Her father, the king, did not even like to have her step into the hall leading to the big front door. Some one might come in and see her.

Now the king was not ashamed of his little daughter. He was proud of her and loved her very much.

But he was a Moslem, and Moslems do not think that men outside of one's family or one's servants should look at a woman or a young girl. So Melanie never went outside of the palace in which she was born, but spent all of her time in its pleasant rooms or in the lovely garden.

Although Melanie had never seen the outside world, she knew a good deal about it. She had a big brother who had gone to school in France and England and who traveled all over the island of Zanzibar with the soldiers who made the laws and collected the taxes. Once upon a time, the sons of kings did nothing but just sit around and have people wait on them, but Melanie's brother was not that sort. He believed that men were happier when they were doing something for others so he tried to learn all he could about his own people and to help them. He persuaded the king, his father, to pipe water down from the hills so that everyone would have all the sweet pure water he wanted to drink and to bathe in. There was less sickness in Zanzibar after that. He also brought doctors to Zanzibar to care for the babies and small children and old people. He had lighthouses built at those points on the coast where there were dangerous rocks. He was always doing some unselfish thing, and the people loved him for it.

"Our island home is the sweetest smelling land in all the world because most of the cloves for English and French and American kitchens are grown here in Zanzibar," Melanie's brother told her. "Why, the breezes from our island are so different from the breezes of other lands that when a boat nears Zanzibar the passengers line up against the rail and sniff and sniff and sniff!" Melanie had never smelled air that was not perfumed with blooming and ripening and drying clove buds.

That was not all Melanie's brother told her. He said that outside the walls of their home, not only in far distant lands, but even on the island of Zanzibar, there were women who went to school and learned to paint and to write books and to cure the sick and to do all sorts of things. He wished Melanie might be such a woman. Melanie wished she might, too.

But the king did not agree with them. He had seen some of these women who painted pictures and wrote books and doctored the sick—and none of them wore black veils over their faces! Did it not say very clearly in the Koran (which is the Moslem Bible) that a woman must veil her face when in the presence of strangers? Therefore, since these women did not veil their faces when they went out on the streets, they were not good women. He would not have any daughter like them!

Then one day the big brother came home with a terrible headache. That afternoon he sat out in the garden in the shade of a sweet lemon tree, but the

next morning he was too ill to get up from his bed. The king sent a servant for a doctor, and after several hours the servant returned with a big woman with short curly hair and a pith helmet on her head. But no veil! The servant was ashamed and afraid to look the king in the face for having brought such a creature to the palace.

"To the soldiers first I went," said the servant, bowing low before Melanie's father, "but their doctor was away on the mainland, shooting the lions for fun! They say, 'Go to English Mission and ask for Doctor there.' I go—but I turn and run when I see this big woman come without a veil! Then I go to French Mission. Same thing there—Doctor not home. He go back to France for a little while. Then everywhere I try to find a man of medicine. Always the same reply: 'Go to English Mission.' I worry and worry, 'fraid young master die, so I go back to English Mission after this shameless creature. I walk with her through all the streets, Allah forgive me! She no cover her face—even when we get here to palace, Master!"

It was the first time such a thing had ever happened! Melanie looked at the woman curiously. Her skin was fair, her hair was light, and her eyes were blue. Aside from that she looked just like Melanie and her mother—or any other woman. There was nothing bad about her!

She knew exactly what to do for Melanie's brother. In a little while he stopped moaning and went to sleep, but he was very, very sick. For days he lay in bed and tossed about and recognized no one. There were days, too, when he was too weak to toss about much. Then Melanie's mother sat beside his bed and never took her eyes off her son.

Melanie's father sat there, too, but he didn't always gaze at his son. Sometimes he stared at his daughter. When he did, his eyes had almost the same look they had when he stared at the soldiers who came to pay him money.

Every day the English woman doctor came and took Melanie's brother's temperature and felt his pulse and gave him medicine. One day Melanie's father followed her to the door.

"Yes," Melanie heard the doctor say, "Your son is very ill."

"But will he get well?" Melanie's father's voice was harsh and deep with grief and worry.

"I'm doing all I can for him," the doctor replied. "As you Moslems would say, whether he recovers or not is in God's hands."

"He is my only son," the king said softly.

"Yes, I know." The doctor had a low voice, and it was warm with pity.

"If he should die, who would be king of Zanzibar after me?" Melanie's father asked.

"You have a daughter," the English woman replied. She and the king looked each other full in the face for a long moment, and then the doctor went away.

The next morning Melanie's brother was much better, and each morning after that he grew stronger. Finally he was sitting up once again under the sweet lemon trees.

The English doctor continued to call at the palace, only now instead of taking his temperature, she laughed and talked with her patient. She had several long serious talks with Melanie's father, too.

One day the king called his young daughter to him.

"Melanie, my child," he said, "your brother had told you of the wonderful things Christian women in the outside world do. That they paint pictures, that they write books and that they become healers of the sick. When your brother was so ill, I learned that they also sometimes become queens. That is, the same as kings, only they are women, of course.

"To serve wisely," he went on as though talking to himself, "one must know the world one governs. One must also know a great many things about other countries. One doesn't get that knowledge in a secluded garden. And the best rulers, Melanie, my child—even those who do not have their laws made for them and their taxes collected by soldiers from another nation!—are those who study the needs of their people and try to help them.

"God grant that your brother be spared to reign as king long years after I am gone. But if he should again fall ill, and if it were to please God to carry him away to Paradise, there must be someone to take his place besides an ignorant, veiled girl."

The king patted Melanie's dark head gently.

"If the English woman should take you to her country to study," he asked Melanie, "would you try your very best to learn everything a good and wise queen who wanted to help her people should know?"

Melanie didn't need to reply. Her eyes shone like twin stars in her face. And because her brother was older and thin from his sickness, his eyes were even larger and brighter stars.

The Jackal and the Honey Bird

Thud! thud! thud! went Hephzibah's feet on the ground—Hephzibah, or the Jackal, whichever you wanted to call her. The girl's hurry was so great that her flying heels hardly touched the ground. And *thud! thud! thud!* her heart was keeping time with her pounding footfalls, for Hephzibah, or the Jackal, had found a solution to her problem. She must find her mother, or father, or big brother—someone to help her with her wonderful solution—before another found it and took it for his very own.

Because she had been born on the trail as her tribe, the Xosas, moved from one pasturage to another, and the jackals had chattered and howled all night long about the camp, the baby girl had been called the Jackal ever since. That is, of course, until she had started to school.

The white woman—who covered her body all over with cloth and even placed a shallow basket upside down on her head whenever she left the shadow of a thatch or other roof—did not seem to like many things this child had been used to. She did not like her to daub her skin with red and white ochre, for instance. She did not like her to stiffen her hair into strange designs with a mixture of castor oil and clay. She did not like the child's only garments to be a bracelet or two of copper wire and a bunch of green leaves or grass tied around her waist with a piece of rawhide. And she did not like a little girl to be called "the Jackal."

The white teacher had taken down her Bible and had searched through it for some suitable name to use instead of "the Jackal," and had finally called her pupil by the Hebrew name *Hephzibah*—which means "delightsome." That described the little girl very well, but it was harsh sounding to Xosa ears, and the Jackal did not know whether she liked it or not. Her mother and father knew, however—they did not! And they did not use it! So their daughter had remained the Jackal to them.

The one whose father and mother called her the

Jackal, was a good student. She learned to understand the strange markings in books almost as quickly as her brother had done—and she learned to cook white man's food and sew white man's clothing even more readily. She had always loved to sing the songs of her native village; and she never had to listen to one of the strange songs of the white teacher more than twice before she knew it by heart—both words and music.

What pleased the white teacher most was that she did whatever she was told with shining eyes and smiling lips. This girl was anxious that those about her be happy and she never seemed to think of sparing herself where their pleasure was concerned.

Hephzibah remained one of the best pupils in the white teacher's school until the rainy season came—when it did not rain! Gardens, which the Xosa people had confidently expected to sprout and cover the ridges and hills with a luxuriant growth, remained mounds and wrinkles on the face of the black and red veld. The seeds lay buried in their little nests of dust as unconcernedly as though they were still tucked away in a earthenware pot awaiting the growing season. They lay, that is, until mice, hundreds of mice, appeared out of nowhere and burrowed into the mounds and ridges. There was no need to kick the earth aside when one saw their holes and lacelike tracks in a garden; the foolishly hopeful person who did, never found anything but crumbled hulls.

At first it had not made such a difference. The Jackal's father and brother had kept the family cooking pot supplied with meat, while the Jackal herself —relieved of the drudgery of continual battle with stubborn weeds—ranged far and wide over the veld, sometimes with other girls, sometimes by herself. She brought home many a huge ball of wriggling furry creatures which gave the family a delicious caterpillar sauce with the evening meal.

After a while the animals began drifting north. Somehow they knew there was water there—that in that direction flowed a great river, with so much water between its banks that it could not run dry in a thousand rainless seasons. At first they seemed merely to drift, feeding delicately on the rattling leaves of the tinder-dry karoo bushes as they went— but headed always in the direction of the great river. Later, when Hephzibah, or the Jackal—whichever you wanted to call her—was thin and listless and only looked without studying at the pages of the book the white teacher put in front of her, there were few animals left on the veld. They were difficult to stalk because all of them were traveling—northward! If the Jackal's father chanced to bring home a hartebeest, or even one of the huge wildebeests, there was never much besides bones inside the flapping skin—no luscious and toothsome fat at all. A little stringy muscle and marrow from the largest bones—that was all.

Then Hephzibah no longer walked across the veld each day to the little group of buildings called a "Mission," where the white teacher had taught her and other Xosa girls to read and cook and sew. Sometimes she thought of those happy days with regret, days packed full of new and strange experiences for her and the others. Most of the time, however, Hephzibah merely lay in the shade, moving only as the cruel sun pushed back the shadows. Occasionally she lifted her head and went through a weak pretense of sniffing, a hopeless gesture for she knew there was no water in the air. There were only the dry stony beds of water courses on the veld, and nothing but the unbroken blue sky overhead. Sometimes she thought of it idly as a bowl, turned upside down on the earth—and the imprisoned people inside roasting, like tiny lizards in a Xosa oven.

Then came the evening—such a short time ago!— when the Jackal's father had awakened everyone within her mother's hut. He did not need to tell them why. With the first conscious seconds, every pair of nostrils had flared, and every pair of eyes had gleamed as the parched lips had murmured their word for "WATER!"

Water! Water! The Jackal had stood in the rain

and rubbed her body all over with a handful of grass—as the white school teacher had taught her to do when there was artificial rain in one of the Mission sheds. It felt good—better than grease and ochre had ever felt. By morning there was a faint tinge of green on the face of the earth. Not all eyes could have seen it! But the Jackal had sharp eyes. She could smell it, too. The veld was alive again. The animals would come back—and presently there would be greens along the banks of the water courses. The Jackal had patted the flat space between her protruding hip bones, and licked her lips and smacked them noisily at the thought.

Hunger no longer abode in their hut, but the days which followed were far from idle for the Jackal and her mother. New seeds had to be planted, and the weeds—without planting—grew ten times as fast as the pumpkins and corn and yams.

As she wielded her hoe and pulled the soft dirt up about each tender plant and shaped and patted each mound with her feet, the Jackal had begun to talk once again of the white teacher in the Mission building just a little way across the veld.

"No," her mother had answered the unspoken question in her little daughter's eyes. "No! Before the dry season lengthened itself beyond our understanding, I dared—I could because we had them!—take from our store of mealies and yams and give to the white woman so you could have a length of cloth to bind about your hips. So you could have all the things she said that you must.

"But there is nothing, now, to give her. Greens from the banks of the water course, we have, and an occasional animal for the cooking pot. Enough for ourselves—but no more! And we are not the only hungry family on the veld, little Jackal. Later, perhaps—some other time—"

The Jackal whacked at the weeds with so much energy that she drove her hoe deep into the earth. So deep, in fact, that it took some wriggling back and forth to get it out again. That was because she knew her mother was right. She must bring something in her hand for what she carried away in her head.

"And there is nothing! Nothing! Not even one little insignificant thing that I can take the white teacher that she will have! If only she would taste a trayful of roasted mice, now, or a broiled puppy dog—but when one mentions these things to her, she turns even whiter than God made her," the Jackal murmured aloud in her hopelessness.

"Tweet, tweet! Tweet, tweet!" came from a karoo bush on the edge of the yam patch as though in answer.

The Jackal leaned on her hoe for a moment's rest and wondered if the little gray bird were a friendly spirit trying to comfort her. Well—if it were a spirit, one must be polite and answer it; and if not, if only a bird, no harm would be done. So the Jackal pursed up her lips and whistled: "Tweet, tweet! Tweet, tweet!"

"Tra-ra-ra-ra-ra-la-la-la-la!"

The little gray bird in the bush puffed up its chest and burst into a perfect rhapsody of song.

And, "Tra-ra-ra-ra-ra-la-la-la-la-la!" answered the Jackal.

Then the bird darted off toward a clump of trees on the horizon. The Jackal followed it with her eyes for a moment and then fell to hoeing. But she had not cleared the weeds away from more than one hill of yams until she heard it again:

"Tweet, tweet! Tweet, tweet!"

The Jackal raised her eyes in astonishment; and there on the same karoo bush sat the self-same little gray bird.

"It must be a friendly spirit—it could be nothing else!" the Jackal breathed to herself. Oh, yes, it must be! And it had appreciated the courtesy of her reply before. She must do the same thing again; and the Jackal pursed up her lips.

"Tweet, tweet! Tweet, tweet!" she chirped so nearly like the bird itself that a stranger would have thought there were two of them somewhere in the garden.

"Tra-ra-ra-ra-ra-ra-la-la-la-la-la!" came in such an

ecstasy of joyous music that it fairly shook the karoo bush.

So, "Tra-ra-ra-ra-ra-ra-la-la-la-la-la!" the Jackal answered without a second's hesitation.

Again the bird fluttered into the air and flew toward the clump of trees on the horizon. This time the Jackal did not go on with her work, but watched its flight. And it did a very peculiar thing. It flew for only a little distance, alighted on a karoo bush, and started twittering. As the Jackal stared, with her mouth actually fallen open, the bird flew back to her a second time, and came to rest on a yam ridge almost at her very feet. It turned its head on one side and stared back at her with a wide-open eye. It looked impatient, almost as though it were saying: "Stupid! How many times must I tell you to follow me?"

Clearly, there must be a spirit in the bird, the Jackal told herself, swinging her hoe over her shoulder and setting off. That satisfied the bird, too, for it never flew more than a short distance ahead of the Jackal before it stopped and waited for her to catch up. On they went, the Jackal—or Hephzibah, if that is what you would rather call her!—and the little gray bird, ever toward the clump of trees on the horizon.

As they neared the small grove, the Jackal noticed a huge old baobab tree in the very middle, its limbs loaded with monkey bread, as she called its fruit. These were sour and a little bitter, but the Jackal's mouth watered as she thought of them. She smiled as she thought of how pleased her mother would be when she returned to the hut with her arms loaded with the pulpy balls.

But the Jackal never carried any of the monkey bread to her mother and father and big brother, for as she stood beneath the huge old tree and peered up into its branches, she saw something which amazed her. An old limb, probably one of the first which had ever sprouted from the hoary trunk (and as big around as the Jackal's mother at her thickest place), had a little hole in it. A simple thing—just a little hole! But in and out of that hole, bees were hurrying.

And so the Jackal's feet *thud! thud! thudded!* on the veld and her heart *thud! thud! thudded!* in her breast as she flew over the ground. She understood everything now. It had not been a spirit which spoke to her, but simply a honey bird. Everyone knows that, since a honey bird loves honey and young bees and yet cannot smoke the hive out of its nest by itself, the bird seeks the aid of men whenever it has found a bee tree. And no native in all Africa would think of robbing a bee's nest without leaving a liberal supply of both honey and young bees for the honey bird.

And the possession of honey— Well! honey was wealth. One neighbor would give almost anything for a potful of honey or a trayful of young bees. Even at the little trading post where white men's things were

to be bought, if one carried a new calabash full of honey, strained ever so clean and clear of bits of twigs and bark and—

The Jackal stopped short so she could grasp more fully the wonderful idea which had just come to her. With a calabash full of such clear, pure honey she'd dare cross the veld once again to the little corrugated iron school house and face the white teacher inside! The Jackal hesitated for only a second, but her feet no longer thudded on the soft earth when she again started homeward. They hardly seemed to touch the ground so quickly she flew to carry the good news.

Smoking out the bees was fun. Her mother and father and their neighbors made a party of it, dancing and feasting far into the night. The honey bird ate its fill out of the store provided for it in a little bark trough and was asleep in the branches overhead long before its human friends thought of slumber. Even the white woman who taught Hephzibah how to sew and cook and read, even she came and enjoyed the fun.

"You are truly a delightsome child," she said to the Jackal. "I named you well when I called you Hephzibah."

"But we cannot say that hard word," the Jackal's father broke in. "The sounds do not come readily from our throats. They are not soft and melodious to our ears. We have a word, *Nanziwe*, which means the same. Or, easier still, why not *Tholba*, which means Joy? For truly our daughter is a joy to us."

"Indeed she is a joy, is she not?" the white teacher asked, although it was really not a question. And when the girl's parents only smiled, the teacher felt fully answered.

"Very well, then," she said after a short pause. "Let us call her 'Tholba'—Joy."

And Hephzibah, or Tholba now, half asleep in the dancing shadows cast by the firelight, smiled. It was to the Jackal that the honey bird had come, to a native Xosa girl, naked except for a few bracelets of copper wire and a bit of grass tied around her waist by a rawhide string. No matter what she learned in the Mission across the veld, no matter how deep her joy in those things, whenever her people were in real need, Tholba knew that she must be as strong and resourceful and persistent as the jackals of the veld.

The Elephant and
the Hippopotamus

It would be nice if we had something to go with the nuts, wouldn't it?" the Hippopotamus asked the Elephant. There was still a long trail ahead of them before kraal and supper.

"Um huh!" answered the Hippopotamus, or something which sounded very nearly like "Um huh!"

"Some caterpillar sauce?" questioned the Elephant, and then hastened on, anxious to please—after all, the effort was costing nothing but words. "Or some honey?"

Of course, the nuts were crisp and good, but *Njamba*—or the Elephant—had had parched peanuts the day before, and the day before that—and for many days previous, in fact! And he wished he had something toothsome—or sweet would be better yet—to go with them. Almost anything would be good: a mango, a custard apple, a handful of dates, or even a small, sour orange from the trees planted by strange white men whom not even the oldest *N'gola*, or smith, could remember now—trees long since run wild.

These *Afulu*—white Christians—there was no understanding them. They were kindly, they fed one; they were generous; and they made long, wearisome journeys across swollen, crocodile-filled streams through the ever-deepening jungle to bring medicine to any N'gola who lay within his hut beset by the devils of pain. But the questions they kept on asking so persistently! Nor did they ever seem to remember the answer given them just the day before.

"I told the Lady Afulu the story of the-people-of-the-spear and the-people-of-the-hoe again today," Njamba said to *Ngeve*, the Hippopotamus, as he sighed heavily.

Ngeve sighed now too—by way of polite sympathy. She, too, the twin sister of Njamba, sometimes found that their teachers were very hard to make understand certain things. Now take that matter of their names. Why should there be any question as to which of the two, brother and sister twins in the land of the N'gola, should be known to men as the Elephant and which as the Hippopotamus? Was not the elephant the larger, wiser and greater animal than the hippopotamus? And was not Njamba—the elephant—larger, wiser, and greater than his sister, Ngeve—the hippopotamus—she being a mere woman?

But the Afulu, besides asking so many foolish questions about the-people-of-the-spear and the-people-of-the-hoe, had a way of turning things upside down that was most confusing. These white Christians who taught them the magic of the "talking leaves"—which they called by the queer name of "books"—had amazed the brother and sister alike when they expected them to leave school each day, if not hand in hand, at least side by side! It had been a new experience for both of them, of course, but the Elephant and the Hippopotamus found themselves enjoying this new and strange companionship very much. Here they were again today sitting down on the old log together, having taken care before sitting down to see that no army of ants hid in the rotten bark ready to pounce upon bare legs and to tear as much skin and flesh as possible from the bones before they could be beaten off. Of course, back in the village, the two would never think of sitting down together on the same log. How could a woman put herself on a level with a man? Nor back in the village, would Ngeve, the Hippopotamus, have received a handful of nuts from Njamba, the Elephant, before he had finished eating his own. In fact, if there were none left for her, she would have had to go hungry—or search the bush on the edge of the village for some wild berries or, perhaps, a handful of nice fat grubs. Ngeve looked now at her twin brother, and her heart skipped a beat just as it always did nowadays when she saw a look of affection there instead of a look of contempt.

"Tell me the story, will you please?" Ngeve asked Njamba. She knew the story as well as her brother; but if he chose to sit and talk with her about anything at all it would prolong the time of this good companionship. A story would mean, too, that the drudgery of pounding corn into meal for mush for her family's supper would be that much further away.

Njamba knew too that, back in their mother's kraal, no one ever listened to his tales with quite the same breathless interest as did his twin sister. It would be more pleasant, too, to tell it to her than to the Afulu who always kept interrupting with their foolish questions. He had learned the proper answer to a lot of them, though. The white Christians were always pleased when you said the simple word: "God." Their favorite question was, "Do you know who made you?" And Njamba had finally found out that the one word was the answer. Of course, there were other questions like: How old are you? What is your name? Where do you come from? Don't you ever help your mother in the garden? The

Elephant flushed with anger at even the memory of this last question they had asked him. Why could they not understand that he, one of the-people-of-the-spear, could not possibly grabble around in the dirt among the roots and weeds? Had he not already explained dozens of times about the beginnings of the-people-of-the-spear and their womenfolk, the-people-of-the-hoe? But like as not, the very next day the same Afulu would ask: "Where did you, the N'gola people, come from?"

"Once upon a time," Njamba, the Elephant, now began, to his sister's delight. He spoke grimly as though he had a kindly, generous, painstaking, but slightly stupid Afulu in front of him—and as though he were determined that this time the story should be remembered! "Once upon a time," he began again with a new breath, "before there were any other people in the world, there was a man and his wife. The man was a *N'gola*, that is, he was a smith—he worked in metals. Now the one great spirit over all nature, plants, rivers, and animals, was pleased with this man and woman, and gave them power over all the earth. The woman had the great happiness of looking at and admiring her husband all day long; while the man had the even greater happiness of making wonderful things in his smithy.

"The man and the woman had never known what

138

hard labor or want were until the day this first N'gola fashioned a hoe. As soon as the broad flat blade was out of the fire and had turned black and cold and its crooked neck had been fitted into a short length of stout thornwood, the hoe began cultivating for them the fruits and herbs and vegetables with which the great spirit had covered the face of the earth for man to enjoy. And immediately the fruits of the soil began to grow larger and more rapidly and much more tasty.

"Then a strange thing happened to the woman: a great desire entered into her heart. She tried to imagine what the fruits of the earth would be like if they were even larger and more luscious. She began to urge the hoe to work faster and faster, telling it to delve ever deeper and deeper into the earth. The man was astonished and fearful of the great spirit's displeasure. He tried to reason with the woman. But who can do that? A woman's lack of understanding has always been!"

The Elephant paused and looked rather sharply at the Hippopotamus sitting beside him. That inferior animal stopped munching peanuts long enough to nod a dutiful, "Oh yes!" The gratified Elephant ate a peanut deliberately, tasting every crumb of its crisp goodness before going on with his story.

"The N'gola, the smith, could do absolutely nothing with the woman. There was more, much more of every kind of food than they could ever eat; but she was as one totally without wits. She shouted and stormed at the hoe, and at last seized it by its thornwood handle in order to show it how it might work harder and faster!

"That was her undoing for, once her fingers were wrapped around the handle, she could not untwine them. Nor did the hoe stop its cultivating; but together, woman and hoe, they whacked and thwacked away at the surface of the earth. The seasons came and went, but the woman's toil did not end. Up and down flew the hoe! Up and down threshed the woman's arms! Up and down pumped her back! Sweat and pain had come into the world. And, because in her desperate struggle to free herself, the woman caused the hoe to slash into good and evil plants alike, many fruits and herbs and vegetables were destroyed—and thus hunger came to mankind.

"Then the N'gola, the smith—the woman's husband—ground his face in the dust at the feet of the great spirit and begged for mercy, lest he and the woman die. At first the great spirit was not inclined to listen to the man's pleading, for he was very angry indeed that the woman had not been satisfied with all the good things he had given her and the man. The great spirit reminded the man that he, being the larger and stronger and wiser creature, should have curbed his wife's desires and directed her conduct.

140

"But the man would not rise from the dust nor leave off his pleading. At last the great spirit wearied of hearing his piteous cries, so he commanded the hoe to cease its labor and to let the woman go. But he said that never after should the hoe work of its own accord; always, when the ground must be broken up around the roots of any plant, the woman must swing the hoe up and down, threshing her arms, and pumping her back like the handles of a pair of the smithy's bellows—with much sweat and pain!

"And so, Ngeve, that is why women must work in the gardens and are called the-people-of-the-hoe among us N'golans."

Again Njamba, the Elephant, paused until the truth of the old story should have time to impress itself upon his sister's mind. And he had not long to wait.

"Um huh!" she agreed promptly, and with eager pleasantness. Had she not known from the time she knew anything at all that women and girls are poor creatures at best? It is true the Afulu—the white Christians—had made every effort to teach her the same magic from their talking leaves as they taught her twin brother. They were always quick to make excuses for her when he outstripped her and covered two bundles of talking leaves while she was still struggling through the first. She had to work too hard at home, they said. She had to carry too much water; she had to pound too much corn into meal; she had to hoe too many hours in her mother's garden. They even went so far as to suggest that Njamba, the Elephant, her brother also wield a hoe amongst the weeds! What could one reply to such folk? People who were so clever and so kind and so generous in many many ways—and yet seemed totally unable to understand some of the simplest facts of life which every N'golan child knew almost from birth.

"Um huh!" Ngeve agreed. She smiled a warm pleasant emphasis into the two grunted syllables.

"And how did men come to be called 'the-people-of-the-spear'?" she urged gently.

The Elephant gave no sign of suspecting that his sister was deliberately prolonging their little visit together. After all, he too enjoyed the flattering attention she paid him—and since the hard labor of smashing a huge basketful of corn into meal awaited her in the village, let her rest a bit, he told himself, before she must swing the heavy pestle, taller than she, into the huge mortar.

"The great spirit was angry with the man because he did not curb the woman's desires," went on the storyteller now. "Still, the man had not done the wrong himself, so it did not seem right that he should be punished. Nor had the man been dissatisfied with what the great spirit had given him; so why should he be humbled? Finally, as the anger of the great spirit

died down, he remembered that the man had been weak only where the woman was concerned—had let her have her way in the first place, and had pleaded for her in the second. So the great spirit decided that the man must henceforth supply the woman with those things she needed and could not get by the labor of the hoe. That is, he must bring her meat for her cooking pot, skins to cover her body, and must protect her from enemies—he must become a hunter and a warrior. And that is how men became the-people-of-the-spear—but there is no shame connected with this work, you understand, Ngeve? For old N'gola, the smith, the first man, did not displease the great spirit who made him, except to beg mercy for his foolish wife."

"Uh huh!" the Hippopotamus agreed, still pleasantly—and wished there were some way of stretching the afternoon out a little longer.

"I wish we had some honey," she murmured. "I wish a honey bird would come right out of the jungle and whistle to us and then lead us to its bee tree."

"Um huh!" This time it was Njamba who grunted assent. He even raised his eyes and peered into the dense green canopy overhead. There was no honey bird up there—but the shade in the tops of the silk-cotton trees was beginning to turn blue. Without a word he slid off the old log and started for their home kraal. Gradually, as they trudged along, Ngeve, the

Hippopotamus, fell behind Njamba, the Elephant. And that was as it should be—she would have been the first to admit that fact. "Is not man superior to woman?" she would have asked. Even as the elephant is superior to the hippopotamus? Whoever among junglefolk thinks otherwise, is a fool indeed!

Dearly Beloved

She was leading a gazelle by a string tied around its
neck when Ned first saw her and the spindle-legged
beast was no shier than the little girl. If the crazy old
Ford, held together by the faith of Ali, its beturbaned
Indian driver, and a liberal supply of baling wire, had
not turned a corner so quickly, Ned would not have
seen her at all. It had seemed to him that she leaped
and whirled in the air almost as lightly as her pet.
Then he had rubbed his eyes and wondered whether
he had actually seen anything at all, for, search the
walls of the massive old ruins as he would, his keen
eyes found no sign of life among the jagged rocks.

"Who is she?" Ned demanded of Ali.

"Oh! Her? *Ayleese?* She is nothing-at-all, of-no-value-whatsoever. She lives here with the Zimbabwe Bantu. She came here with Ibrahim, the dioula," the Indian driver had replied carelessly.

" 'The dioula—the dioula!' " Ned's father had exclaimed as he hung on to his seat in the jolting car. "What tribe is that? I never heard of them before."

Now Ned's father was an engineer who knew all about the rocks on and under the surface of the earth, but his lack of wisdom in the practical things of life amazed Ali a dozen times a day.

"What tribe is the dioula!" he snorted in reply—not at all under his breath—and twisted his body to stare at his employer. Whereupon the creaking Ford shot off almost at right angles to the direction in which it had been traveling! If there had been ditches at the side of the road or fences and fence posts, there might have been tragic results; but since there wasn't even a road to begin with, and the great Zimbabwe ruins lay on the other side of the car, it didn't really matter.

"The *dioula*—they no tribe at all," he explained as he turned again, this time forward. "They Arab traders who travel all over Africa. Long ago they came in caravans, and they were armed. Then what they wanted most was slaves. If the Bantu—or any other tribe—said 'No' to selling their young men and women to the traders, they seized them anyway. But the Arabs could pass all over Africa. It was only from them that people could get the things they had learned to want: mirrors, knives that were hard and strong and sharp all at the same time, and so on.

"But times are changed now. Little slavery—except in the deepest parts of the forest. Who is sure what goes on there? Not even the dioulas, who go everywhere with their packs of things both for black people and the white settlers now, know all that goes on in a jungle village."

The Indian driver turned his rattletrap car into a gateway and stopped with a jerk. Ned and his father were at home at last—at home after a long ocean voyage of many miles and many days from New York to the eastern coast of South Africa. With every mile on their drive inland, there had been something new and strange and wonderful to be seen. The distance had seemed short: a cheetah crossing the road with one bound; a lion sunning itself on a rock, and only raising its head to look curiously at the car as it passed; a herd of giraffes rocking across the veld like floating hobby horses; and monkeys popping up everywhere! As Ned stood at the foot of the steps of the cottage in which he and his father would live while his father worked as overseer of the Zimbabwe gold mines, New York and America seemed very far away indeed.

Then, as day followed day, Ali made a much better guide for a boy's rambles than he did a driver of the car. He knew everyone who worked at the Zimbabwe mines—"white sahibs," as he called Ned's father and the other Americans, as well as the shivering black boys who disappeared down the gaping mouths of the mines every cold dawn. Better still, he knew the names of all the birds and animals which flitted over the plains. He knew the native villages—and the people in them—from which workmen for the Zimbabwe mines came. He knew strange tales about the Zimbabwe ruins whose massive walls sprawled over many acres of land.

These ruins were a continual source of wonder to Ned. He liked to explore the moss-covered tunnels and open passageways, to clamber up to the very peak of the south tower which stood like a faithful sentinel guarding the inner courts. Looking at the stone cubbyholes, he tried to imagine what kind of homes they must once have been. Up there, atop the tower, Ned could see not only for miles across the veld, but even more of the ruins below.

It was thus he saw her for the second time. She was seated on a block of stone which had tumbled from a near-by wall. She was weeping bitterly. Her gazelle lay across her knees with its nose resting on her forearm—like a sleepy puppy dog. Ned held his breath as he pointed her out to Ali—as he would have held his breath had she been a rabbit, or a squirrel, or some other timid woodland creature. But Ali did not share his caution. Instead he shouted down to the little girl—"Ayleese! O-o-o-oh, Ayleese!"—and after a startled glance upward, she had disappeared once again, her gazelle still in her arms.

"Ayleese? She is nothing—of-no-value-whatso-ever!" Ali almost snorted. Then he went on to explain to his worried listener. "She came here with Ibrahim long time ago now. Ibrahim was one of the dioulas, who visited us here in the Zimbabwe territory once a year. We all knew Ibrahim and liked him. He always tried to find out what everyone wanted so he could bring it with him when he came the next year. He camped each time in the Bantu village. Some people say that he took a Bantu woman away and married her—but I don't know. That was before I came to Zimbabwe. Anyway the last time Ibrahim came, he brought this little girl, Ayleese, with him; and he left her with the Bantu while he went into the bush to trade with the tribes there. He expected to come back—everyone says he said he would come back. But he didn't, and no one knows why. Maybe Ayleese his daughter—but how is one to know such things?

"What could have happened to him? Oh—a thousand things! A lion, a snake, even one of the big apes, maybe—"

"Perhaps he lost his way," suggested Ned.

"Eh? No-o-o-o! He never got lost! Not Ibrahim! The dioulas know Africa better than—well, at least as well as—the Africans themselves. No! No one ate him! How could that happen? There are no cannibals in this part of the country any more! He met with some sort of accident, for no word about him ever came back to the Bantu. By the time people realized something was wrong, it was too late to look for him. Here the birds and the beasts eat up all flesh; the ants turn the bones to powder, and bush and vine cover up everything else.

"And Ayleese? She stays. She belongs to no one. No one belongs to her—but only her little gazelle. No one denies her a bite from a cooking pot. And she sleeps where she may. She is a-thing-of-no-value-whatsoever!"

And that was all Ali, the Indian driver, seemed to know about Alice—or "Ayleese," as he called her.

But the next time Ned saw the little girl, they both stood what would have been face to face if she had not bent her shy head so far that he could look down the back of her neck and even under the top folds of the strip of calico she wore loosely twisted about her thin body. Her gazelle turned its great sloe-colored eyes from person to person, and sniffed anxiously like a puppy whose master is in danger. The skin on its neck and shoulders quivered, although no flies were there to dislodge.

Now Ned had talked to his father about Ayleese—had supposed this and that and the other thing about the shy creature and her gazelle until his father became curious about her, too. Ali was persuaded to guide Ned and his father to the Bantu village where Alice lived more like one of the wild creatures of the veld than a human being, but he was full of scorn the whole way. The dioulas were privileged men, "Yes," he admitted—and often immensely wealthy. But was not Ayleese only a girl child? As such she was the lowliest of the low, he spat out. And now that the man to whom she had belonged—as daughter or slave, it made no difference!—had disappeared into the bush and failed to return—— Ali spread his hands wide in helpless questioning: Why should one concern himself with such a poor creature? It was very clear that Ali, who could enjoy doing nothing for days on end, thought all this visit to the village a sheer waste of time.

But Ned's father asked questions of the village chief, of the young huntsmen of the village who had known and liked Ibrahim, the dioula, and of the women who missed his visits to the village—and the beads and mirrors and copper wire for necklaces, and the many, many other things he had once brought with him. At last, Ned's father tried to question the shy Alice herself, but she only dropped her head

153

still farther and would not answer him with a word. Only the little gazelle pointed its nose anxiously at first one and then the other of the human beings around them, looking at all with sad and troubled eyes.

That night Ned's father decided to write two long letters. One he addressed to the Sultan of Zanzibar, and the other to the British Consul in the Sudan. Before posting them, he said to Ned, "Practically all of the Arabs who peddle merchandise of any sort throughout Africa have come from one of those two countries. Surely we'll hear something that will help solve this puzzle."

Ned's father had reasoned that, if Ibrahim, the dioula, were from one of those two places, either the Sultan or the Consul would know about him because he was well aware of the fact that it was from them that peddlers must receive permission to carry on their trade.

About three weeks later—a long time it seemed to Ned—a reply came from the Consul, but it told them nothing more about Ibrahim. They waited and waited. At last after many weeks came a letter from the Sultan of Zanzibar. They started to read it eagerly. It was very formal, of course, and devoted several paragraphs to elaborate greetings. Finally the Sultan got around to explaining about an old man with an empty heart, who lived in an empty house in the city of Zanzibar on the island of Zanzibar. In his youth, it seems, this old man had been a *dioula*, a peddler, and had amassed great wealth thereby. His son had followed in his footsteps. He also had been successful and had added to the great fortune of his father—who was and would remain the head of his own and his son's households as long as he lived.

The Sultan's letter went on to say that the old man's name was *Abou Ibrahim*. Ned and his father both looked up from the letter and smiled at one another, for they knew that that meant, "Father of Ibrahim." Now they read on, eagerly.

Ibrahim, the son, traded with the Bantu in the Zimbabwe territory on the mainland. One day he brought home with him a beautiful young girl from the village on the edge of the great-ruins-about-which-men-talked-much-but-knew-little. He had made this girl his wife. Later on, they had a child born to them. The infant was only a girl, and, therefore, of no more value to the family of Abou Ibrahim than any slave, but she was a very beautiful child. The years only added to her beauty and grace, so they called her "Alice"—the Princess—and she was much loved by everyone, especially by Abou Ibrahim and his son, her father.

In fact, the-little-thing-of-no-value-whatsoever—but so fondly called the Princess—was no more than able to toddle about on her two stubby legs when the father began begging her grandfather for permission to take her with him on one of his trips. Abou Ibrahim had replied, "No!" emphatically! A peddler's journey was a long and hard one. There were wild beasts, stinging insects, and strange sicknesses in the lands he must penetrate. Furthermore, there were many miles, long weary miles where cart and carrier were not to be had, and he must depend on his own legs and strong back. No! A dioula's, a peddler's pathway was not for childish feet; and so Ibrahim had departed alone.

But the next year—and the next and the next and the next—Ibrahim had asked the same question—had asked for so many next years that Abou Ibrahim wearied of saying, "No!" and finally had dropped his head and had murmured, "Take the child."

The old man had given her a tame gazelle so that she might not miss the companionship of other children on her long trek. His last memory of her was with the little beast muzzling her plump thigh as the two stood in the stern of the boat which carried them away from the city of Zanzibar on the island of Zanzibar to the mainland of Africa.

Although my old friend (the Sultan's long letter ended) lives in a palace crowded with many people— friends, relatives, servants—among whom there are many children, his house is empty, as is his heart. If you will send his granddaughter back to us, all the wealth which men call mine, I will lay at your feet when you touch the island of Zanzibar.

"Does the Sultan mean he is going to give us everything he owns?" Ned asked. "Really give it *all* to us?"

"No-o-o-o!" his father laughed. "Oh no! That is just a very polite way of saying 'Thank you!'—and of telling us that he wants us to visit him sometime."

The prospect of a visit—especially to a real Sultan—thrilled Ned all the way down to his toes. He could think of nothing else as, a few days later, he stood on the pier and watched the big boat pull away with Alice and her soft-eyed gazelle gazing at him from the top deck. Now he saw her only as the Princess Alice going where she would no longer have tears in her eyes, where she would be truly as rich as a princess in the love of those about her. Ned and his father and Ali, the Indian driver, were standing together there on the pier.

Ned heard Ali sniffing loudly, "Ayleese, a-thing-of-no-value-whatsoever!" He hoped the boat was far enough away for her not to hear.

But the next moment his heart sang because of his father's whispered remark. It was something about not being driven in a Ford to see the Sultan! Ned could hardly wait for the time of the visit to come.